It's Not All Roses

Maia Terry

Contents

	VI
	VII
1. Rosalind	1
2. Rosalind	6
3. Atticus	9
4. Rosalind	12
5. Atticus	16
6. Rosalind	19
7. Atticus	25
8. Rosalind	32
9. Atticus	36
10. Rosalind	39
11. Atticus	44
12. Rosalind	47
13. Atticus	50
14. Rosalind	53
15. Atticus	57

16.	Rosalind	62
17.	Atticus	65
18.	Rosalind	69
19.	Atticus	75
20.	Rosalind	80
21.	Atticus	86
22.	Rosalind	90
23.	Atticus	93
24.	Rosalind	97
25.	Atticus	101
26.	Rosalind	104
27.	Atticus	108
28.	Rosalind	112
29.	Atticus	117
30.	Rosalind	123
31.	Atticus	130
32.	Rosalind	134
33.	Atticus	139
34.	Rosalind	143
35.	Atticus	147
36.	Rosalind	150
37.	Atticus	154
38.	Rosalind	158

39. Rosalind	162
40. Atticus	166
Acknowledgments	169

Trigger Warnings

This book contains explicit language and mature themes that may be triggering to some. These include mental health topics such as panic attacks, PTSD, depression, self-harm, attempted suicide (mentioned briefly), alcohol use (mentioned briefly), physical and mental abuse, and off-scene, sexual assault.

To my younger self, I hope you're proud.

Chapter One

Rosalind

Two Years Prior

I can't believe I let Amelia drag me to this game. It's not that I hate basketball, I actually enjoy it. I'm just not in the mood to pretend to be upbeat and happy right now. However, after the fight I had with my mom this morning, I know that staying at the house wouldn't be the smartest move.

"Earth to Rose." Amelia waves her hand in front of my face, grabbing my attention.

"Sorry, I spaced out," I say, turning to look at her. "What were you saying?"

"I was just telling you how I wanted you to meet Trevor tonight," she says with a smile.

Trevor is the guy she has been talking to for a few weeks. I've never seen her act like this over a guy before, so that in itself makes me intrigued to meet him.

"Oh shoot, I knew I should've brought my interrogation notebook," I tease.

Amelia smacks my arm with the back of her hand and turns her attention back to the game. Now that the star player is no longer a red shirt, our school has one of the best basketball teams in the conference. No one knows what happened or why he got red shirted to begin with. Of course, like with any campus, there were plenty of rumors flying around. But no one could back up the claims.

At the sound of the final buzzer, the crowd jumps to their feet, cheering for yet another victory. While people mill about and the players head to the locker room, Amelia and I wait in the stands. Once the majority of the crowd has gone, the guys begin trickling out of the locker room. Amelia squeals and climbs down the bleachers as she sees Trevor. Following behind her we come to a stop at half court.

"Rose, this is Trevor," Amelia says as she introduces us.

"It's nice to meet you, Trevor. I've heard a lot of good things about you." I give Amelia a wink and she groans in embarrassment.

"Hey, Trev. Do you want to go to Tony's? I'm starving," a voice from behind me says, interrupting our conversation.

"You guys okay with that?" Trevor asks as he looks between Amelia and me.

"I love Tony's," I say before turning to the man behind me. I fight to keep my jaw from dropping.

The man behind me is none other than Atticus Reed. I try to be subtle as I take in his appearance. He is a good six inches taller than me, with curly brown hair and the bluest eyes. Tearing my eyes away from his face, I notice the tattoos that decorate his left arm and appear to vanish under his cut off.

"Hi, I'm Atticus," he says with a smirk, clearly catching me looking at his tattoos.

"Rosalind, but you can call me Rose," I reply with a smile.

"Nice to meet you, Rose," he says before looking over my head at Trevor. "Let's go, I'm starving."

Once we arrive at Tony's, we find a booth at the back of the restaurant. Amelia and Trevor slide in on one side, leaving Atticus and me to sit on the other side. I smile sheepishly as I slide in, and Atticus follows.

"What kind of pizza does everyone like?" Trevor asks.

"Meat lovers," Atticus and I say at the same time, and I laugh.

When the waitress leaves after taking our order, Trevor and Amelia instantly fall into a conversation clearly lost in their own little world. I look over at Atticus who is already looking at me. I feel my cheeks flush and I advert my gaze just as the bell dings. My eyes follow some of the other players on the team as they mill by our table, letting Trevor and Atticus know they played a good game. I notice a few of them from class, but I realize I don't know any of them by name.

"You guys coming to the party tonight?" One of the players asks as he comes to a stop at the end of our table.

"Nah, thanks for the invite, Murphy. But we are just going to hang out and eat some pizza," Atticus replies. When he says Murphy, the name clicks. Derek Murphy. I've heard it announced several times during games.

"Oh, come on," Derek says. "I've got some kegs coming, and there's going to be beer pong."

"Oh look, here's our food," I interrupt as the waitress comes up to the table.

Derek grumbles as he walks away, and Atticus looks at me. "Sorry if you wanted to go. I didn't mean to answer for you."

"I don't do parties, so it's totally fine," I assure him and grab two slices of pizza.

As we eat, the four of us make small talk. It's amazing how the conversation just flows between us. I never make friends this easily, but it seems like Trevor and Atticus are the missing puzzle pieces for Amelia and me.

Once we are finished eating, we sit and talk for another hour before we exchange numbers and Amelia adds us all to a group text. I'm actually sad to see the night end.

On the drive home, Amelia glances over at me. "How did you like Trevor?" she asks nervously.

"He made a good first impression," I answer, giving her a reassuring smile.

Amelia lets out a relived sigh before putting her car in park in front of my house. "Thank goodness."

"Be careful going home," I say as I get out of the car. "Make sure you let me know when you make it home," I remind her before shutting the door.

Walking up the sidewalk, I realize that my mom's car is gone. She must be working another late shift. Typical. Anything she can do to avoid me after our fight. I unlock the door and go inside, making my way upstairs to my room. Stripping out of my clothes, I throw them in the hamper and walk to the bathroom, turning on the shower.

When it's finally warm enough, I climb in and sigh as the warm water runs over my body. I close my eyes and lean my head against the shower wall. After a few moments, I grab the shampoo and begin to wash my hair. Once I rinse all the soap out, I reach for my razor out of habit.

I started self-harming almost two years ago, after my dad left. My mom decided that it was all my fault and has spent the last two years making sure I didn't forget it. So, for the last year and a half, this has been my routine. With a sigh, I look down at my razor and let everything else disappear.

After I get out of the shower, I make sure to tend to the fresh wounds on my thigh before I dress and climb into bed. Grabbing my phone off the nightstand, I scroll through the group chat that has been blowing up for the last twenty minutes and smile.

Atticus: I'm thinking we need to go bowling tomorrow night if everyone is free.

Amelia: Oh, I love bowling. I'm free.

Trevor: Hell yeah, man.

Sign me up. Bowling is my favorite.

Thus, the tradition of Friday night pizza and Saturday night bowling was born.

Chapter Two

Rosalind

Present Day

"Hey, Rose," Derek calls as I stand to leave our biology class.

Ugh, not again. I think to myself before turning around and flashing him a smile. "Hey, Derek. Excited for the scrimmage tonight?"

"You bet," he says, coming to a stop in front of me. "I was wondering if you'd like to hang out after?"

"Oh, I would, but I can't. I have plans already," I lie.

"That's what you always say," he says, his smile dropping instantly. "Why won't you just give me a chance?"

"I've told you countless times, Derek. I'm not interested," I say before pushing past him.

He reaches out and grabs my arm before leaning close to my ear. "When will you realize that Atticus wants nothing to do with you?" he growls. "Nonetheless, you'll come around. They always do."

"Please let go, you're hurting me," I whisper as I struggle against his grip. Glancing around, I notice we are the only two in the room now, but the next class should be coming in soon.

He releases my arm and I hurry out of the room, not looking back. Seeing my group of friends in the distance, I pick up my speed and throw on my signature smile as I try to shake off the feeling of Derek's hand on my arm.

"There she is," Atticus says, throwing his arm around me. As he does so, my mind goes back to what Derek said. *Do I want Atticus to want me?*

"We were just talking about what we are doing after tonight's scrimmage," Amelia says with a smile as she loops her arm into Trevor's.

"Oh, I can't do anything tonight guys. I have a biology test tomorrow and even though finals are over, it's still a big portion of my grade, so I need to study," I say with a frown.

The other three look at me with displeased faces. "What a party pooper," Trevor teases.

I roll my eyes at them and shrug. "Sorry, some of us have goals after college, Trevor."

"Your words. They wound me." He puts a hand over his heart and frowns.

"Alright, alright. That's enough, you two," Atticus says before letting out a soft chuckle. "I have to get to class, but I will see you at the scrimmage at least, yeah?" he asks with a hopeful smile.

"Absolutely," I promise, before waving goodbye to him. Trevor and Amelia leave not long after that and since I have the rest of the afternoon free, I head to the library to get some extra studying in.

My phone buzzes on the table as Amelia's name pops up on the screen. "Hey, I'm leaving the library now," I tell her in a hushed voice as I pack up my books.

"Hurry up, it's getting chilly out here," she whines on the other end.

"Oh, it's not that cold." I say as I walk to my car. Putting my books inside, I tell Amelia I will be right there and shut my car door. It's a perfect night out, so I decide to walk instead of driving my car over to the athletic center.

When I arrive, I find Amelia standing outside, shivering. "It's about time," she says as she breathes into her hands.

"You are so dramatic," I say as I roll my eyes and laugh. "Come on, wouldn't want you to get frostbite."

We find our usual seats and watch the boys warm up. Not long after we are settled in, the game begins. The crowd cheers as the guys score point after point, with Atticus being the lead scorer. Time seems to fly by and when the final buzzer sounds, our team walks away with their second victory of the season. Even though this was a scrimmage, everyone treats it as though it was a regular game.

Checking the time on my phone, I look over at Amelia, who is still seated. "I'm going to head on out," I say as I lean down to hug her.

"Okay! Be careful on your way home," she says as her eyes scan the players walking out of the locker room, obviously searching for Trevor.

"I will. Tell Attie I said good game and I will call him later." I turn and walk down the bleachers, before walking out into the cool night. While Amelia was exaggerating earlier about how cold it was, it is unusually cool for Tennessee this time of year.

As I'm passing the science building, I get the feeling of someone's eyes watching me. I glance around nervously but see no one, so I shrug it off. Just as I walk past the alley between the science and arts buildings, someone reaches out and grabs my arm, pulling me into the alley.

As my eyes adjust to the sudden darkness, they grow wide as the person who grabbed me comes into focus. Derek's hand is on my throat before I can even make the first sound.

Why didn't I wait on my friends?

Chapter Three

Atticus

Man, does it feel good to be in bed. I sigh as I sprawl out under the covers, scrolling through my phone. Even though it was a scrimmage, it was a tough one. I decided to stay back and take a shower before heading home. When I came out of the locker room and Amelia told me that Rose had left early to finish studying, I was a little bummed.

Coming across Rose's contact, I pull up our conversation. She told Amelia she would call me later but has yet to do so.

> **How's studying going?**

I send and wait for those three bubbles to pop up. After a few moments, there's no reply and I raise my brow.

> **Missed you after the game. I'm sorry I took so long to get out of the locker room. Next time I'll skip the showers.**

> **It's okay. I'm fine. Really tired. Going to head to bed. Goodnight.**

> **Okay... goodnight, Rose. Sweet dreams.**

That's odd... she is never that short with me. Is she mad? I'll have to pull it out of her tomorrow. Sighing, I place my phone on charge and before I know it, I'm drifting off to sleep.

The next morning, the incessant beeping of my alarm pulls me out of my sleep. Rolling over with a groan, I hit snooze and lay in bed, staring at the ceiling. The day after a game is always the worst. I'm tired, both physically and mentally. All I want to do is sleep.

However, my scholarship is dependent on my grades and my status on the basketball team. I may be the star player, but I have academic expectations to uphold as well. I'm constantly reminded that life isn't just basketball, even though for me, it is. Its what earned me a full ride to Savanna University.

Climbing out of bed, I go to my closet and skim through my clothes. Once I find the jeans and sweatshirt I was looking for, I change and then head to the kitchen to grab myself some breakfast. After making a mental note that I need more groceries, I swipe a banana and a bottle of water off the table and head out the door to class.

Pulling into the parking lot, I head toward the area where our friend group usually parks. Trevor and Amelia are here already, but it doesn't look like Rose is. Glancing at the time on my phone, I frown. She's never late, and our professor is strict on arriving in a timely manner. I lean against the side of my Jeep as I wait for her.

After five minutes, it doesn't appear that she will be arriving soon, so I head on into the building. Making it into the classroom with five minutes to spare, I find my usual seat and check my phone one more time to make sure Rose hadn't texted. Sliding my phone back in my pocket after seeing no new notifications, I let out a sigh.

The professor begins his lecture, and about ten minutes into it, Rose walks in. Professor Graham gives her a look and then continues his lecture. When Rose sits down beside me, I turn to look at her, the lecture long forgotten.

Taking a moment to really look at her, my brows furrow. She has a smile that could light up any room that she walks into. I look forward to seeing that smile every single day. Today, though, she seems anxious. She is chewing on her lip, and her eyes are darting around the room every so often. She begins to fidget with her fingers. One of her tells that indicates her anxiety is rising.

In an attempt to calm her, I place my hand on top of hers, but it causes her to jump, and she pulls her hand away. There's no denying the hurt that flashes across my face, and I slowly pull my hand away. When she notices what she's done, she gives me an apologetic look and then turns her attention to the professor.

For the rest of the class, I try to focus on the lecture. It seems impossible though, because my mind is running a hundred miles an hour trying to figure out what is going on with the strawberry blonde beside me. When the professor finally dismisses us, Rose rushes out of the room.

Grabbing my books, I follow her. "Hey, Rose…" I say as I catch up to her. "What's going on? Why are you avoiding me?"

She glances over at me and shrugs. "I'm not. I just had a long night studying."

"Right…" I say, trailing off, leaving nothing but uncomfortable silence between us as we walk toward our next classes. We are in different ones, but mine is in the same direction, which gives me time to pull something out of her. "I've known you for two years, and I have never seen you in a scarf," I say, trying to make some type of conversation.

"I wanted to try something different," she snaps as she pulls the scarf tighter around her neck and I let out a sigh. Clearly, she doesn't want to talk to me.

"Okay, well, I will see you after class," I say as I turn to go in the direction of my class.

I have no idea what is going on. She says she's fine, but I call bullshit.

Chapter Four
Rosalind

It's almost dismissal. It's almost dismissal. I chant to myself repeatedly. This is my last class of the day and then I'm free. My fingers are sore from clenching my pencil so tightly today while I've tried to keep it together.

With last night heavy on my mind, I glance over at Amelia, who is already looking at me with her face scrunched in confusion. I quickly look away from her and pretend to be writing something down.

My friends have done nothing to deserve the rudeness I have been giving them all day, but I can't help it. If I tell them what happened, they will all lose it. I can't deny that my heart broke a little when I saw the look on Atticus' face after I flinched away from him. He definitely didn't deserve that, but it was just instinct.

I adjust my scarf quickly, afraid it may have shifted. I can't let anyone see the bruises on my neck. If they do, questions are going to fly and that's something I absolutely do not need. The hair on the back of my neck rise and the all too familiar feeling of being watched creeps in. I don't even have to look in his direction to know who it is. Derek has been staring at me throughout the entire lecture.

I shouldn't have come to school today, but I need to keep up my grades if I'm going to graduate with my bachelor's degree on time. Finally, the professor dismisses us, and I quickly grab my supplies before bolting out the door. The second I'm out the door, I head to the bathroom.

I run my fingers through my hair as I stare at myself in the mirror. "You're fine. You're safe. The day is over," I repeat to myself in a whisper over and over. Once I've gotten my heart rate under control, I gather my things and head out. As I turn the corner outside the bathroom, I run straight into a solid wall of muscle.

"Oh, I'm s-" I start to apologize, but then I lock eyes with the person I bumped into, and my blood runs cold.

"Well, if it isn't little Rose," Derek says with a malicious smile. His dark brown eyes have me rooted to the spot. "Where did you run off to so quickly? You left poor Amelia dumbfounded," He teases.

"I need to go. I'm late for class," I lie as I sidestep around him, but I'm not quick enough because he cuts me off and I step backward, so I'm pinned between him and the wall. The familiar scent of his cologne instantly takes me back to last night. My heart begins to race as I fight back tears.

"Remember what I said, Rosalind. Not a word to anyone. I can ruin you. I can ruin Atticus," He hurls the same threat he said last night.

"I haven't said a word. Now please let me through." I'm determined not to let him see me cry. He doesn't deserve the satisfaction. "Derek, let me through." I whisper and try to move past him. Surprisingly, he lets me through, and I walk like I'm heading to class until I'm out of his line of sight.

Speed walking to my car, I unlock the door as I approach. A hand on my upper arm causes me to jump out of my skin. "Please, st-" I begin to say whirling around. Once I see who it is, I slouch against my car. It wasn't Derek. Just Atticus. "I'm sorry, I thought you were someone else," I breathe out.

"Are you okay? You look like you've just seen a ghost," Atticus says as he looks down at me, his tall frame towering over mine.

"Yeah, you just scared me." I look away from him. I don't know if I can keep it together if I look into those ocean blue eyes.

"If you say so," he says with a shrug. His phone alerts him of a new text and I look up at him as he pulls it out of his pocket before glancing down at it. Not that it's any of my business, but I find myself watching his expression in hopes that it gives away to whoever he's talking to. "It's Trevor," he says, looking back down at me, running his hand through his thick curly brown hair. "He wants to know if we want to join him and Amelia at Tony's?"

His hopeful eyes search mine, waiting for an answer. I chew my lip before looking at my watch. "Yeah, okay. Let's go," I say with a nod. I could really use some time with them.

The excitement that crosses his face adds a little light to the darkness that has been my day today. "Awesome, I can drive," he tells me before he opens the door for me. I was in survival mode this morning when I arrived, and I didn't even notice that he was parked beside me.

Climbing into the passenger side, I immediately connect my phone to his Bluetooth and turn on my current favorite song, "Control" by Zoe Wees. He never says anything when I take over the music, which I love, he just lets me do my thing. You can tell a lot about my mood based on whatever music I'm listening to at that point in time. On my darker days, Atticus tries to cheer me up by remixing some of the songs into a happier version.

This time, however, Atticus looks over at me with a raised eyebrow. "Are you sure you're okay, Rose?"

"Yeah, I just really like this song," I mumble while avoiding his gaze. I busy myself on my phone, scrolling mindlessly through social media. My stomach is turning with nerves. Atticus isn't dumb and I will only be able to keep up this lie for so long before he figures it out.

Atticus would do anything for me, which is why I hate keeping things from him. But once he finds out, he is going to fly off the handle. I need to tell him. I know this, I just don't know how. I just can't come out and say, "Oh yeah, by the way, your teammate, Derek, assaulted me after the scrimmage last night." Thankfully, it's almost winter and the cool air makes it easier to hide the bruises under long sleeves, pants, and scarves.

Looking over at him, I find myself smiling softly as he sings along to whatever song was in the queue after my first pick. Becoming friends with Atticus was not in my plans. But after Trevor introduced us, it didn't take long for us to become inseparable. Soon you didn't see one of us without the other. I go to all his ball games in support and when he's not in the gym, he keeps me company during all my insane marathon study sessions.

As if he can sense me thinking about him, he quickly glances over at me. He gives me his dazzling smile, causing my heart to race before he turns his attention back to the road. *Damn him and that smile.* We've been friends for two years now, and it still blows my mind that Atticus Reed wants anything to do with me.

He's the star basketball player for Savanna University. Girls are constantly throwing themselves at him. He's always getting invited to parties. Me? Well, I'm a nobody. Boys aren't falling at my feet. I don't party. The only thing I have going for me is my grades.

Atticus clearing his throat snaps me out of my thoughts, and I realize we have made it to Tony's. When I glance at Atticus, his blue eyes are already locking on mine. I try to hide the blush that creeps onto my face, but his smirk tells me he noticed.

"Wow, Trevor and Amelia are here already," I say as I look past him to where the couple is standing. "Let's not keep them waiting," I add, as I quickly unbuckle and slip out of the car.

Chapter Five

Atticus

When I'm finally done with classes for the day, I head out to the parking lot. Smiling as I see Rose walking to her car, I jog up to her and put my hand on her arm. Just as I'm about to speak, she whips around, in the middle of telling me to stop touching her. I step back and put my hands up. "Woah, it's just me."

She apologizes, saying she thought I was someone else, and then proceeds to slump against her car. The relief is visible on her face, and I wonder who she thought I was. "Are you okay? You look like you've just seen a ghost?"

She quickly replies that she's okay and just as I'm about to press further, I get a text message. Pulling my phone out of my pocket, I glance at the screen. It's Trevor wanting me and Rose to meet him and Amelia at Tony's.

After Rose agrees to go, I help her in the Jeep and then climb in. Once I'm out of the school parking lot, I notice her music choice. Interesting. "Are you sure you're okay?" I ask her. She quickly tells me she's fine, and the way she avoids my gaze tells me she wants to drop it.

We pull into Tony's in silence because she hasn't said a word since I asked her about her song choice. When I look at her, she's lost in thought, so I take a moment to study her face. What is going on in that pretty head of hers? It's clear she's stuck somewhere deep inside her head, so I clear my throat. That seems to pull her out of her thoughts. I want to ask her about it, but right when I open my mouth, she quickly points out Trevor and Amelia, then rushes out of the car.

Sighing, I get out of the car and follow the three of them inside. We walk in and head to our usual booth, and I slide in beside Rose as the server comes over to grab our drink orders. She must be new because we are here so often all the staff know our usual order.

"So, Trevor, have you gotten cleared from the doctor yet?" I ask after we have ordered.

He groans and shakes his head. During the first game of the season, he took a brutal charge, smacking his head on the floor as he went down. It earned him a nice concussion.

"That's bullshit man." The doc has been taking his sweet time releasing him, but we have the biggest game of the season coming up and we need him.

"Come on, Attie," Rose says as she places her hand on my arm. "You know, the doctor just wants to make sure he is in tiptop shape before he releases him." It's hard to focus on her words because her touch sends a tingle up my arm. When did this happen? When did I start to fall for the beautiful girl sitting beside me?

She's not wrong though and luckily, I don't have to admit that because our pizza comes out. For the rest of the meal, we make small talk, talking about the most recent game and our plans for winter break. Usually, we host a tournament, but Coach decided this year we deserved a break. Taking advantage of the time off, Trevor, Amelia, Rose, and I are all heading up to my family's cabin this weekend after tomorrow's game. It's been a while since the four of us have been able to go to the cabin, and I can't wait.

Throughout the conversation, I take note that Rosalind is quieter than she usually is. Amelia keeps talking to her, and she gives one-word answers or unenthusiastic replies. Halfway through the meal, Amelia gives me a look that says she is concerned. I'm glad it's not just me and that someone else is noticing the difference. It seems like she's always looking over her shoulder every time the door jingles with a new customer.

As if on cue, the bell above the door goes off, and Rose looks back at the door. I feel her stiffen beside me and I turn around to see what has caused the change in her behavior. Derek Murphy and his friends just walked in, which is nothing unusual. They're here almost as much as us.

Derek makes his way to their usual table and greets us as he walks by. Rose sits her pizza down and pushes her plate away. Amelia's eyes find mine again, and I give her a subtle nod. I'm going to have to have this uncomfortable conversation with Rose, whether I like it or not.

Once our food is gone, we say our goodbyes to Trevor and Amelia and then make our way back to my Jeep. When we're inside, I turn to look at Rose, not even bothering to start the Jeep. I don't want her to feel like I'm trapping her, but I also don't want her running away this time.

"Rose," I say gently.

"Yeah, Attie?" she murmurs as she reaches over to buckle her seatbelt, not looking at me yet.

Reaching over, I tuck a piece of hair behind her ear before giving her a small smile. "Are you okay?"

"I'm fine," Rose answers quickly, with a smile that doesn't quite meet her eyes.

"You know you can always tell me anything," I say and reach over to grab her hand. She flinches away, but quickly recovers as she takes my hand in hers. I play it off like I didn't notice, but she was never like this before. It's not like me placing my hand over hers is anything abnormal. The last few months, there have been more and more rumors going around about us being together. I've been waiting to make my move, but now, my focus is on finding out what's going on with her.

Chapter Six

Rosalind

Hearing Atticus' sincere offer to help me, I nod. "I know, Attie." After a few seconds, I clear my throat. "My mom is expecting me soon." I lie, and he nods, defeat clear on his face.

Dropping my hand, he sighs heavily. "Let's get you back to your car then." He says as he starts the vehicle. His words are laced with disappointment. I know he wants to be there for me. I just don't want to drag him into the darkness, too.

The drive back to my car is quiet, neither of us really having anything to say. Once at my car, he squeezes my hand again. "I mean it, Rosalind. No matter what time it is. If you need me, I will be here. Call me anytime day or night and I will show up at your doorstep." I know he isn't kidding because he's done it before to Trevor. He was having a tough time after he and Amelia got into a fight, and Atticus showed up at two a.m. just so he could be there for him.

Nodding, I lean over and kiss his cheek. "I promise I will call you if I need you," I say before I exit his vehicle and get in mine. I don't even remember the drive home because I'm so lost in my thoughts. Sitting in the vehicle for a few moments before letting out a scream of frustration, I hit the steering wheel with my palm. "Fuck!" I scream out. "Why me?" I ask through unshed tears.

After a few more screams, I blink away the tears and get out of the car. After saying a quick hello to my mom, I head to my room. My body is buzzing as I rush up the stairs. I've been on edge all day and mix that with the minimal amount of sleep I got last night, I'm ready to call it a night. Attie didn't know what was happening when he started questioning me, but it brought back the memories I've been trying to erase for the last twenty hours.

Walking into my bathroom, I turn on the shower and quickly undress. I stare at my reflection as I wait on the water to heat up. My gaze falls to my legs and as I take in the sight of the self-inflicted wounds on each thigh, a tear slides down my cheek. Wiping it away, I climb into the shower, exhaling with relief as the warm water rushes over me.

As soon as I let that breath go, the dam breaks and tears start falling. They continue to fall as I think about the disappointment in Atticus' voice when I avoided talking with him, the sincerity of his concern, but more importantly, they fall for the girl who died last night, and the girl she is becoming.

After I finally climb out of the shower, not having it in me to do anything other than wash my hair and body, I throw on my favorite comfort pajamas and settle into bed. I try to distract myself from my racing thoughts by scrolling through social media. It doesn't help. Going to Atticus' name in my phone, I hesitate but decide to call.

"Rose," he says as he answers. "I was just thinking about calling you."

"Hey Attie," I whisper softly. "I just wanted to call and apologize for how I acted today. I've just not been in the best mood, and I took it out on you and the rest of the group. I'll apologize to the others tomorrow, but I couldn't sleep without apologizing to you."

"Honey," he begins, that pet name he's been calling me lately causing butterflies to flutter in my stomach. "I know that something is going on with you, but I promise that whatever it is, you don't have to go through it alone. So please don't shut me out."

Blinking back tears and trying to keep my voice steady, I begin to speak again. "I know… I just need some time to process everything."

"Is it your mom?" he asks.

"It's always something with her," I say as I let out a dry laugh. "I'm just asking that you be patient with me, please."

"Of course," he promises. "I'll be here when you need me, Rose."

"Thank you, Attie," I whisper. "I guess I will let you go to bed. I'm pretty tired myself."

"Okay, I will see you in the morning. Goodnight and sweet dreams, Rosalind," he says before disconnecting the call.

I sigh and roll over, grabbing the melatonin that lives permanently beside my bed and take three in hopes they'll help. It's not long after that when I drift off to sleep.

A nightmare crushes my hopes of getting a good night's sleep when I wake a few hours later. I was back in the alley, and Derek had just pinned me against the wall, his hand around my throat.

My head is pounding, my chest is so tight I feel like I can't breathe, which causes me to panic even more. My hand goes to my chest as I try to take deep, calming breaths. After a few minutes, I'm able to calm myself down and I lay staring at the ceiling for the rest of the night. Every time I close my eyes to go to sleep, I see his face.

At seven a.m. sharp, my alarm clock goes off, signaling it's time to get up and get ready for class. I sigh heavily and make my way over to my vanity, looking in the mirror. "Wow, it's going to take a lot of makeup to cover these dark circles." I mutter as I brush out my hair. Making my way over to my closet, I grab a pair of sweatpants, and one of Atticus's sweatshirts I have lying around. I don't want to wear a pretty shirt and scarf today, so I put some concealer on my neck and am able to cover the bruises with foundation. It's not perfect, but it's good enough that no one should be able to tell.

Once my hair and makeup are done, I head down to the kitchen to grab a granola bar and water. The house is eerily quiet, and I assume that my mom has already gone to work. That's nothing new though, she's always working. We see each other twice a week, but honestly, it doesn't bother me. Our relationship is anything but perfect and I'd rather avoid her as much as possible.

When my dad left us 5 years ago, my mom became distant. She projected her anger for him onto me, even though I had nothing to do with him leaving. Being treated like you're nothing at fifteen really does a number on your emotional state. It's not my fault he caught her red-handed with her coworker.

Dad was supposed to be at work when she brought him home on their lunch break. Dad came home early because he wasn't feeling well and caught them. It wasn't long after that before his bags were packed, and he left. We talk here and there, but I haven't seen him in a few months. With our schedules, it's never really a good time for either of us.

Heading outside, I jump into my car and turn on my "Bad Bitch Time" playlist before driving to school. Even if I don't feel like a bad bitch, I have classes with Derek today, so I need to put on a brave face. To say it'll be hard to be in the same class as him is an understatement. However, having Atticus and Amelia around makes it a little easier, even if they don't know they're doing anything.

After parking in my usual spot, I glance at the clock and realize I have about 10 minutes to make it to class before the professor gets pissy. Luckily, I should be able to make the trek in six. Grabbing my books and my purse, I jump out and make my way to class.

Apparently, everyone and their brother are late to class this morning because it takes me the full 10 minutes to arrive. My eyes land on Atticus as I make my way through the rows of seats in the lecture hall. After our conversation last night, I feel a little better about everything that happened, and the smile on his face tells me that he has put it behind him.

"Well, well. Look what the cat dragged in," Atticus teases with a grin. "I didn't think you would make it before Mr. Stickupmyass started."

"Yeah, apparently no one wants to go to class today. There were so many people heading into other classes late," I mumble back as the professor walks in. "I don't blame them, though. It's the Friday before winter break." Usually, colleges have finals the last week before the holidays, but we have ours the week before and then all the professors make us come for no reason the following week.

"You're still coming to the game tonight, right?" Atticus asks as he gives me puppy dog eyes.

My stomach churns at the thought of going to another ball game, especially with Derek being on the team. But if I'm going to keep up the façade that everything is okay, I have to act as normal as possible. Normal Rose wouldn't miss one of Atticus's games. So instead of declining, I nod my head. "I wouldn't miss it for the world."

I'm looking down, writing some things in my notebook that were already on the board when I hear Atticus greet someone as the seat beside me moves. After finishing my sentence, I look up and freeze suddenly, all four walls closing in on me.

"Hey Rose," Derek says as he claims the seat beside me.

"It's Rosalind." I grit out, impressed with how strong my voice sounds.

"Literally no one calls you Rosalind." Atticus says behind me. Getting angry at him is pointless, because it's not him getting under my skin, so I push my annoyance down and shrug.

"I'm asking him to call me Rosalind," I snap, putting extra emphasis on 'him'. Atticus gives me a weird look, but thankfully, I'm saved from any more interaction because the professor begins the lecture.

All throughout the lesson, I can't concentrate on anything that's being said. All I can focus on is the fact that Derek is less than 5 feet away from me and I am about to crawl out of my skin. Feeling impatient and anxious, I start gathering my supplies, ready to bolt as soon as the professor says it's time to go.

As if he can sense my apprehension, Mr. Hugh ends the lesson and wishes us a good winter break. I immediately stand and push my chair back in. "Attie, I will see you after our next class," I say as I rush out of the room, not giving Derek a second glance.

Walking toward my next class, I take deep, calming breaths. I know that I should go to this class because attendance is necessary, but I can't face Derek without one of my friends with me today. So, instead of doing so, I take a left and rush to the parking lot.

I'm not feeling well. I didn't get enough sleep so I'm going to head home and take a nap.
Amelia, I will meet you outside the gym before the game.

I send the text to the group chat with Atticus, Amelia, and Trevor before pulling out of my parking spot and heading home.

Chapter Seven

Atticus

Furrowing my brows when I get the text from Rosalind, I look over at Amelia and hold my phone up. She shrugs and then turns her attention back to the professor. She's worried but not *as* worried about Rose as I am, but I don't see how. It's obvious that something is wrong with her. I could tell by the way she spoke to Derek when he sat beside her in our first class. I'll have to meet up with him before the game, to see if he has some answers.

This class drags by so slowly. It's like the universe is drawing out our last class before winter break. The ball game tonight is the only thing standing between me and spending the weekend at the cabin with my friends. The professor dismissing us brings me back to reality. She dismissed us 30 minutes early and I smirk assuming that everyone was too rowdy for her to want to bother keeping us here any longer.

Heading to the athletic center, I shoot Rose a quick text.

Hope you're doing okay. We got out early, and I'm heading on over to the gym to warm up for the game.

I will be there. Good luck. I can't wait to see you after!
Huh, a sudden change from earlier.

Once inside the locker room, I change into my uniform and throw my warmup on. There are a few guys already milling about, but my eyes zero in on one in particular. "Hey Derek, you got a minute?"

"Yeah man, what's up?" he asks as I come to a stop beside him.

"Did you notice how weird Rose was acting this morning? She seems to really have it out for you. What was that about?" I question, studying his face. I've never seen Rose act like that toward someone. I can't help but wonder if he's the reason she hasn't been acting herself or if he is just caught in the crossfire.

"Oh man, you know. She tried to come on to me after the scrimmage, and I turned her down because I'm talking to Ashley. She must not have taken it easy." Derek explains as he busies himself with tying his shoe.

What? That makes no sense. She never expressed any interest in Derek to me. Trust me, I would have known about it because unfortunately Rose is very open with me when it comes to her dating life. Plus, Amelia said Rose went straight home after the game.

Instead of replying, I turn my attention to Coach, who just walked in and is beginning to discuss what he expects out of us tonight. His usual speech. All I can focus on is what Derek said. After Coach finishes talking, everyone disperses to finish getting ready. I keep as much distance between Derek and me as possible.

"Atticus Reed has done it again, ladies and gentlemen," the sportscaster booms over the speakers after I sink another three-point shot, pushing us to the lead by one point just as the buzzer goes off. The crowd cheers as we shake hands with the other team and head to the locker room.

"Good game, Reed," Derek says as he walks by my locker. I give him a grunt and finish changing into my regular clothing before grabbing my bag.

"Hey man, you ready?" Trevor asks as he walks over to my locker after the session ends. "Amelia said she and Rose would be waiting for us outside."

"Yeah, I'm ready." I shut my locker and follow Trevor outside.

When we find the girls, I notice the look of distress on Rose's face as she looks around. It's like she's searching for someone, but the moment her eyes land on mine, it seems to lessen, and she gives me a smile.

What has her so on edge? First the interactions with Derek yesterday at Tony's and the one this morning, and now this? I have a feeling Derek was lying to me when he said Rose came onto him.

"Great game, Attie," Rose says as she jumps into my arms and gives me a hug.

I catch her effortlessly and chuckle. "You say that after every game," I tease.

"Yeah, and I always mean it." She wiggles out of my arms, and I set her down on her feet gently.

"You ladies ready to go?" Trevor asks as he takes Amelia's hand.

"I just need to stop at the house and grab something I forgot," Amelia says and Trevor groans.

"Woman, you would forget your head if it wasn't attached to your neck," he grumbles before turning to walk to his car. "We will meet y'all there."

As Rose and I walk to my jeep, I look over to see her practically bouncing down the sidewalk. I swear she is the cutest thing I've ever laid eyes on. I didn't really get a chance to take in her outfit this morning, but seeing her in my hoodie that she stole from my house a few weeks ago brings the biggest smile to my face. Even though Derek said she came onto him, her wearing my hoodie says otherwise.

As we near the car, I hear a familiar voice coming from behind us. Rose hears it too because she immediately tenses up and gravitates closer to me. *Is she afraid of Derek?* She reaches over and slides her arm into mine. I glance over at her, and her expression is neutral, but the grip on my arm says she is definitely not okay.

I glance behind us and notice that Derek is walking our way. Rose follows my gaze and then turns back around quickly.

"Hey guys," Derek yells after us.

The grip Rose has on my arm tightens, and I bite my tongue to keep from making a noise as her nails dig into my flesh. I slow our pace but don't stop as Derek comes up beside us.

"You all coming to the party tonight?" he asks, keeping his eyes on Rose instead of me.

"No, we aren't," I say, repeating the same answer I always give him. "We already have plans this weekend." I'm highly aware of Rose practically shaking like a leaf beside me, and I remove her arm from mine. She looks at me bewildered before I place my arm across her shoulders and pull her against my body. "If you'll excuse us, I'm taking my girl out of town. See you at practice next week."

Once we get to the car, I open Rose's door, and she practically jumps in and tosses her bag into the back seat. Eyeing her suspiciously, I shut her door and get in on my side. "Are you sure that you're feeling better?" I ask her as I back out of the parking spot. "We can cancel the weekend and stay home if you want?"

"No, there's no need to cancel. I didn't sleep well last night, so I guess I just needed that little extra nap earlier," she said with a forced laugh as she buckles up. "I feel much better. I'm ready to get this weekend started."

"Me too," I say as I turn on some music and turn the volume down low so that we can still have a conversation. It's an hour and a half drive from the campus to the cabin, so we usually get comfortable and just enjoy the ride. I look over at her after a moment. "So, I heard something interesting about you today... and I'm not so sure I believe it."

"Oh, yeah?" she says, looking away from the window and over at me. "What's that?" she questions curiously.

"I didn't know you had a thing for Derek." We've always been open with each other, so I hadn't thought anything about bringing this up. But as the color drains from her face, I immediately regret it.

"Where did you hear that?" she asks as she starts to pick at the skin around her nails.

"I had mentioned how it seemed you were upset with him this morning in class, and he said it was because he turned you down." I reply with a shrug.

"Please don't ever ask him about me again," she whispers before looking back out the window. "I don't have a thing for him. He's lying. I just don't get good vibes from him, that's all."

I nod, internally berating myself. Clearly, this is upsetting her, and I don't want to make it worse, so I just drop it. After a tense moment, I peek at her out of the corner of my eye and see she's still picking at her fingers. I sigh and reach over, placing my hand on top of hers, relieved when she doesn't flinch this time. "I'm sorry, Rose. I won't mention him again," I promise her as I lace my fingers with hers and bring her hand up to kiss the back of it.

The ride to the cabin is quiet, aside from us singing along softly with different songs as they come on. Once we arrive, I hand the keys to Rose and tell her to go on in while I grab the bags. Trevor and Amelia haven't arrived yet, which is fine. They shouldn't be too far behind us.

After taking our bags inside and to their respective rooms, I head to the living room to see where Rose has run off to. The cabin isn't huge, but it's big enough. There are five bedrooms, three bathrooms, a den, a dining room, kitchen, a pool house with a hot tub, a movie room, and a game room.

"Rose?" I call out, looking around. Her favorite thing to do is look at the stars, so she's probably out on the porch. Just like I figured, I find her leaning against the railing of the balcony, looking out at the sky above.

Smiling softly, I leave the balcony door open and stand beside her. The early winter Tennessee air sends a chill through me.

"It's beautiful, isn't it?" she says with a big smile.

"It sure is," I say, looking down at her. She thinks I'm talking about the view, but really, she's what's beautiful. Her brown eyes meet mine as she looks up at me, and her smile grows even more. *Man, how am I going to survive this weekend?* Every time I'm around her, I want to just pull her into my arms and kiss her.

Without thinking, I reach out and brush a piece of hair away from her face. "I've missed that smile of yours," I murmur. "It's so nice to see it again."

"I've missed it too," she whispers as she leans into my touch.

"Last time I touched you, you pulled away from me…" I mention as I wrap my arms around her.

"I know, I don't have an answer for you. All I can do is apologize," she whispers as she wraps her arms around my waist. She turns to look over her shoulder as the front door opens.

"We're here! Are y'all naked?" Amelia yells through the cabin. She is always saying things like that around us, not so secretly hoping we will get together. But we have never really talked about taking our relationship to that level, even though I'm feeling increasingly inclined to have that conversation with each passing day.

Rose laughs and goes to meet them in the living room. "You guys sure took your time."

"Yeah, someone took his sweet time getting home and showered, and then taking me to my house to get my other bag," Amelia says as she plops down on the couch, pulling Rose down with her. "I'm starving. What's for dinner?"

"Since it's already so late, I'm just going to whip up some chicken and broccoli with cheese sauce," Rose says as she stands back up and walks into the kitchen. "If someone wants to come and make the cheese sauce, that'd be great." She calls over her shoulder before she disappears into the kitchen.

"I'll go help her. You guys set the table and get the movie room set up for afterwards," Amelia says, as she bounces off into the kitchen shortly after Rose. Trevor and I groan, but quickly straighten up when Amelia turns to glare at us.

"Yes, ma'am." Trevor says as he nudges me toward the dining room.

Chapter Eight

Rosalind

Thirty minutes later, Amelia and I place dinner on the dining room table. The boys are like ravenous animals as they pile their plates high. Laughing, I grab a plate and put some chicken and broccoli on it, before smothering it in cheese sauce.

"I hope you guys enjoy it," I say before I pick up my fork and dig in. Dinner goes by quickly and quietly, with only the random appreciative grunts and mumbles from the other three at the table. After dinner, the boys cleaned the kitchen while Amelia and I go change into our comfy pjs so we can settle in for movie night.

With my pjs on, and my hair down from the bun I'd been wearing all day, I check to make sure my bruises aren't showing, then go to meet everyone for the movie. Grabbing my favorite blanket, I flop down in my designated spot beside Atticus and snuggle close to him. "What are we watching?"

Atticus looks down at me after putting his arm around my shoulders. "I don't know. Some movie Trevor picked." Amelia and I groan at the same time. "Yeah, that's what I said too," Atticus says with a laugh.

Halfway through the movie, Atticus pulls me closer and absent-mindedly runs his fingers through my hair. My body's first response is to shrug him off, but I stop myself before I do. *It's Atticus. You are safe. He won't hurt you*. I repeat to myself in my head as I lean into his touch and let out a content sigh.

The movie wasn't as bad as the ones Trevor usually picks. This one was an action adventure, but it also had a bit of romance, which went well for both parties. Somewhere toward the end, I found myself nodding off to sleep. The next thing I know, Atticus is gently shaking my shoulder.

"Hey, Rose, wake up," He whispers in my ear. "It's time for bed."

"Oh, did I fall asleep?" I mumble before quickly wiping drool off my cheek. I blush with embarrassment.

"Yeah, but it's okay. So did the rest of us. I think the movie has been over for about an hour," he replies, glancing at the clock.

"Damn. We must have been tired," I say with a laugh. I stand up slowly and stretch my arms above my head. "I'm beat. I think I'm going to go on to bed. I will see you in the morning," I say and lean down to kiss his cheek. "Good night and sweet dreams."

"Good night, Rose. Sweet dreams," he says, and I smile at him. We started saying that to each other every night last year, and it's just stuck between us. I turn, grabbing my blanket and make my way up to my room. Climbing into bed, I crawl under the covers and quickly fall back asleep.

I'm pinned against a brick wall, and all I can feel is pressure on my throat. I can't breathe. I need to breathe. I'm struggling. I try to scream, but it comes out strangled.

"Shh, little Rose," says the voice that haunts my dreams and my reality. "We wouldn't want Atticus to find out, would we?" "No, please don't. Atticus..." I cry out.

"Rose. Rose. Rosalind." I'm pulled out of sleep hearing my name.

"What?" I ask and as I open my eyes, I find myself staring at the most concerned pair of ocean blue eyes I've ever seen. *Oh no.* I've had a nightmare.

"You scared the shit out of me." Atticus says as he drops his head and rests his forehead on the side of my bed as he continues to kneel on the floor. "I didn't know what was going on in here. You were crying and yelling my name."

"I'm sorry. I didn't mean to scare you." A few tears must have fallen during the nightmare, and I wipe them away as I mumble. "It was just a nightmare." It's at this moment that I'm aware Amelia and Trevor may have heard me as well, but there's no sign of them.

"Are you okay?" He asks looking back up at me. "I left Amelia and Trevor down in the basement earlier, so they didn't hear a thing," he says as he follows my gaze to the door.

"Yeah, I'm okay... I'm sorry I woke you." I whisper, looking over at the clock. It's four a.m. and I feel absolutely awful for waking him. "Will you stay?" I ask shyly and look down at the bedsheets.

"Of course I will," he whispers, and I pull the covers back for him to get in. As he climbs in the bed, I smile softly, and my body moves closer to him. I throw the cover over both of us, lay my head on his chest and use my fingers to outline the tattoos that decorate his body. As I lay there, I realize how oblivious I was to the fact that Atticus is laying in my bed, shirtless, and I'm just cuddled up to him like it's no big deal.

"Don't apologize for waking me. I'm glad I was able to wake you and pull you out of it. I couldn't make out what you were saying other than my name, but whatever was happening, I'm sorry." He adds, before kissing the top of my head. He rubs my back as we lay there in silence. I'm not sure when, but I must have fallen asleep because the next thing I know, the morning sun is beaming through the blinds.

I go to sit up, but I realize I can't move. Looking down, I see an arm wrapped around my waist. *What the-* I begin to wonder before the events of last night come back to me. I had a nightmare and Atticus brought me out of it. I turn over and find him already awake and looking at me.

"Good morning, Rosalind. Sleep well?"

"Truthfully, when I fell back asleep after the nightmare, it's the best sleep I've ever had." I answer him. I'm vaguely aware of him running his fingers through my hair. Closing my eyes again I sigh contently and lay my head back on his chest. "Thank you for staying with me." I whisper.

"You don't need to thank me." He said as he lifts my chin to look in my eyes. "I will always be here for you." He adds.

Looking into his blue eyes, I find myself getting lost in them. I've always loved his eyes. Aside from his smile, they are one of my favorite attributes of his. My gaze drops to his lips as I chew on my bottom lip. *Man, do I want to kiss him.* As if reading my mind, I watch as his lips turn up into a smile. My eyes go back to his, and he brings his free hand to cup my cheek, rubbing it with his thumb.

Instinctively, I lean in closer to his touch. What would happen if I kissed him? Would it ruin our friendship? *Fuck it.* I will never know if I don't go for it. Scooting to where our bodies are flush against each other, I reach up and place my hand on the back of his neck. Pulling his face close to mine, I smile slightly as I feel him closing the gap between us.

Chapter Nine

Atticus

My mind has been racing since Rose pressed her body against mine, and now I can't hold back. It's been months of wondering and wanting. I can't wait any longer. I need to feel her lips on mine. The second our lips meet, I can't think straight. I cradle her head, pulling her impossibly closer. My other hand slides down to her hip, holding her against me.

Time freezes, and all I know is the soft feel of her lips and the shaky breath she lets out as I hold her close. *I could kiss her forever*, I think, but after a moment, I reluctantly pull back for air. "Rose…" I whisper as I rest my forehead against hers. "You have no idea how long I've wanted to do that."

Rose giggles softly, reaching down and grabbing my hand before lacing our fingers together. "I feel the exact same way," she says before leaning up and pressing a peck against my lips. We lay there silent for a few minutes before Rose speaks again. "So, I hate to be that girl… but what does this mean for us?" she asks timidly. "Friends don't kiss like we just did," she adds with a smirk.

"Well, I guess it means it's time to put all those rumors of us dating to rest," I say with a shrug, trying not to appear anxious. "If that's okay with you." I add quickly.

The smile that crosses her face takes my breath away more than the kiss did. Her dimples are showing and it's the first genuine smile I've seen from her in two days. "Completely fine with me. You already called me 'your girl' when you were declining the party invitation last night."

I feel like a thirteen-year-old boy who held hands with his first crush. All I could think about lately was making her mine and look at us now. Unable to help myself, I lean down and kiss her soft, silky lips again. I only pull away so I can check the time. Groaning, I pull her closer, not wanting to let go. "We better head downstairs, or Trevor and Amelia may come looking for us."

"Let them come look for us. Amelia may have a small heart attack when she sees us in bed together," she muses.

After a few more stolen kisses and promises of coffee, I am finally able to get her out of bed. We walk hand in hand down to the kitchen. Raising my eyebrows at the empty space, I peer down at Rose.

"That's odd," Rose says before she looks out the window. "Trevor's car is gone too," she observes, propping her hands on her hips. "I'll see if I can reach Amelia."

I nod. "I'll make your coffee and bring it out to you if you want to go sit on the swing," I tell her, smiling when she shoots me an appreciative look. Rose is already on the phone with Amelia, as I grab some mugs and get the coffee started. I watch as she walks away. I can't help myself. Man, she is beautiful.

After I finish the coffee, I join her outside on the porch. "Everything okay?" I ask as I sit and hand over her mug.

"Well, her sister is in labor, so she is on her way to the hospital. She said she was going to leave a note but forgot," she shrugs, sipping her coffee. "So, it looks like we have the cabin to ourselves for the rest of the trip."

I give her a small nod before taking a sip of my coffee. "I bet she's excited for her sister."

"She's super excited." Rose turns to look at me. "So... what do you want to do today?" she asks with a raised eyebrow.

"I was thinking maybe going to the pool, or chilling in the hot tub for a bit, and then watching a movie we will actually enjoy. Maybe I can kick your ass at some pool, too?" I offer with a teasing smile.

Rose laughs, it's no secret that I suck at pool. "Sounds like a plan. Let me get changed and we can get in the hot tub. After finals last week, a good soak sounds lovely," she says as she downs the last of her coffee and then kisses me on the cheek before walking away.

After dropping my cup off in the sink, I head up to my room to change into my trunks. When I'm ready, with a couple of towels taken from the bathroom, I head for the hot tub. "Come on, slowpoke!" I yell to Rose as I pass her room. She's shuffling around in there, clearly still changing, so I keep moving.

Making a pit stop in the kitchen, I grab two bottles of water and head on to the hot tub. Turning on the jets and placing my towel to the side, I set the drinks down in the cup holders. Stepping into the water, I slowly sink down, letting it rush over my sore muscles. I close my eyes, leaning my head back to relax in the hot water. It's not long after that when I hear Rose coming, so I pop one eye open. "Took you long enough," I tease. My face falls as I see she is still in regular clothing. "Why aren't you in your bathing suit?"

"I forgot it," Rose says, avoiding my gaze. I furrow my brow. Rose avoiding eye contact is pretty much the equivalent of her screaming 'I'm lying.'

"You have spare bathing suits here," I say, scanning her face. The look she gives me is full of dread, causing me to sit up straight. "What's going on, Rose?"

"I've got a migraine. It just came out of nowhere, so I'm going to take a hot shower then go lay down," she says before she disappears back into the house, leaving me puzzled.

Chapter Ten

Rosalind

Halfway into changing, I realize that if I go down there in a bathing suit, my cuts and bruises will be on display. *Fuck.* I can't let him see me like that. So instead of changing into my swimsuit, I put my pajamas back on and head down to the hot tub.

He looks peaceful, and I know the water would feel amazing on my sore muscles. I just can't bring myself to do it yet. When I tell him I'm not getting in, I'm overcome with guilt because of the disappointment on his face. Great Rose, you're ruining this, and it hasn't even been 24 hours.

Once in my room, I grab my shower bag and head to the bathroom attached to my room. Getting everything out of my bag, I sigh as I think about Atticus. I don't know how to make him happy while keeping him in the dark about Derek.

Jumping in the shower, I close my eyes as the warm water runs over me. My mind is clouded with a hundred different thoughts. Instead of facing my problems, I create even more by disappointing the one person I never want to let down. Sure, I'm overthinking it. It's just spending time in the hot tub. But what's going to be next? What am I not going to be able to do because of the fact that I have been keeping this secret from him?

Staring at the razor on the side of the tub, I chew on my lip. *Why not add another thing to the 'Why you're a disappointment' list?* Reaching out, I take the blade in my hand and add another familiar wound to my collection. I scoff at the thought as tears sting my eyes. A collection. Calling it that sounds like something you'd want on display. This, however, is something I never want to share.

Getting out of the shower, I dry off, clean the wound, and then take a look at myself in the mirror. The bruises are changing colors, and the cuts from a few nights ago have started to heal slightly. I reapply make up to my bruises to hide them and then go lay down.

After my "nap" which was really just me laying in the bed with my back to the door and staring at the wall, I go downstairs to find Atticus stretched out on the couch scrolling his phone. Walking over to him, I take his phone and sit it on the coffee table, before throwing my leg across his waist and straddling him, his hands immediately go to my waist. I bury my head in the nape of his neck. "I'm sorry I didn't get in the hot tub," I mumble into his skin.

He rubs my hip with his thumb and kisses the top of my head. "It's okay, we have all weekend," Atticus says softly. "Are you feeling better?" he adds, and I nod. His hand trails from my hip to my thighs and I flinch as he runs a hand over my newest cut.

"Are you okay?" he asks, pulling his hand away.

"Yeah, I just cut myself shaving," I lie, but he nods, believing the lie. My stomach churns as I internally scold myself for lying to him yet again.

We lay there quietly for a few moments before I sit up and look down at him. "Let's go play some pool," I say before I stand and grab his hand, pulling him with me toward the basement. "Loser does the dishes."

After a full four games of pool, Atticus hangs his head in defeat. "Dish duty sucks, man," he groans.

"Oh, cheer up, at least when the dishes are done, we can veg out on the couch or something and you can have some more of these," I say as I lean up and place a soft kiss on his lips. That seems to light a fire under him as he turns and takes the basement stairs two at a time. I follow behind him, walking like a normal person, and laugh.

Since it's Saturday night, we ordered pizza, and there aren't a lot of dishes thanks to the paper plates. From my seat on the counter, I watch as he cleans off the last coffee mug and places it in the drying rack. I jump down from the counter, and he comes over to me.

"I could get used to seeing you doing those dishes," I tease as I run my hands up his chest.

"I bet you could," he says as he moves closer, pinning me against the counter.

My brain automatically goes into overdrive. Pushing on his chest, I close my eyes but quickly reopen them. "Atticus, please get off," I whisper.

"Rose, what's wrong?" he asks. He shifts to the side, and I'm able to get out from between him and the counter.

"I just can't do this right now," I breathe out as I rush out of the room to the porch, slamming the door behind me.

I don't know how long I'm outside, but the air is getting cooler, and the sun has set. I'm half surprised and half unsurprised that Atticus hasn't come to check on me.

With a sigh, I stand from the swing and make my way back into the house. "Attie..." I call out into the dimly lit room.

"Over here," he replies from the kitchen.

Heading into the kitchen, I see him sitting at the table looking down at his hands. "Rose, what happened?" he asks before his eyes snap to mine.

"I'm sorry, I just freaked out a little..." I say as I sit beside him, looking down at the table.

"A bit?" he scoffs, with his eyebrow raised. "Rose, you practically bolted when I got close to you."

"I just..." I look back up at him with tears in my eyes. "I'm sorry."

"I don't know what else to tell you, Rose," he says with an exasperated sigh. "I know that something is wrong, but you won't let me in. Damn it, why can't you just tell me?"

"I just can't, Atticus. Stop badgering me with questions and I will fucking tell you when I can," I practically yell as I stand from the table and turn to walk away.

His hand shoots out and grabs mine before I walk away. "Wait. I'm sorry, baby," he mumbles. "I'm just used to being able to help you with whatever is going on, and now I feel completely in the dark."

"Let's just go to bed," I say, changing the conversation and slipping my hand from his. He gives me a nod and stands from the table before following me to the bedroom.

Once in the bed, he turns over to me and places his hand on my hip. My back is to him, so he leans up and kisses my cheek. "Good night, Rose, sweet dreams," he whispers.

"Good night, Attie, sweet dreams," I reply before closing my eyes and drifting off to sleep.

When I wake the next morning, I hear the soft snores of Atticus behind me, his arm wrapped around my waist, holding me against him. Looking over at the clock, I am amazed to see that it's eleven forty-five a.m. Slowly climbing out of bed, I tiptoe out of the room to the bathroom. I look at myself in the mirror and then check the bruising on my neck. *Shit.* I need to add more makeup.

After making sure the bruises are covered, I go downstairs to the kitchen to make some coffee. Once it's done, I grab my favorite blanket and walk out to the porch swing. Careful not to spill the coffee, I sit down and get situated before I start slowly swinging back and forth.

The view here is amazing. We are up on a mountain with views as far as the eye can see. Even though it's winter, the snow hasn't reached us yet. When it does, though, it's breathtaking. Hopefully, during one of the off weekends, Atticus and I can sneak back up here. Even if it's just an overnight trip. Last year, things were so busy we only got to come here once.

As I swing, my mind drifts off to last week and how I don't know how I'm going to keep this secret from Atticus much longer. I have to make myself not flinch away when he kisses me sometimes and when it inevitably happens, I want him to be able to understand. My hand goes up to rub the back of my neck, and I sigh, leaning my head back and closing my eyes.

I'm so lost in thought that I don't even hear the door open, but feeling someone looking at me causes an uneasy feeling in my stomach, and I open my eyes. "Geeze, Attie. Warn a girl next time," I breathe out.

"Sorry, Rose, I thought you heard me. This door isn't exactly quiet," he muses before kissing the top of my head.

I slide over to give him a little more room to sit, since I was practically taking up the entire swing. "How did you sleep?"

"I slept pretty well, how about you?" he questions as he gets comfy beside me.

"I slept really well," I answer honestly.

"I wonder what changed?" he teases as he nudges my shoulder with his.

Everything. That's what changed.

Chapter Eleven

Atticus

Hearing her say that she slept great last night makes me so happy. I don't know why she hasn't been sleeping well, but I'm glad that she was able to do so in my arms. I noticed that she looked more rested too, which is great. As I sat down on the swing beside her, I let my arm drape across the back of the swing.

Last night was strange, and I wish that I could get her to talk to me. I could pry, but I know better than to push Rosalind Johnson. So, I will just have to wait until she is ready to come to me.

"I'm glad that you slept so well, angel," I say as I lean down to kiss her temple. She blushes slightly and rolls her eyes.

"Moving on to the pet names, are we?" she says with a quirked eyebrow.

"Absolutely. I'm wasting no time here." I nod with a flirtatious grin.

"I can tell," she says with a laugh. Rose leans over and rests her head on my shoulder as we swing back and forth, enjoying the quiet while admiring the view.

After sitting on the porch swing soaking up our quiet time together, I look down at her. "You want to hit the hot tub with me one more time before we have to go?" I ask. She usually loves the hot tub, so it surprised me when she ditched me yesterday.

"I told you I don't have a suit," she says, sitting her coffee cup in her lap, irritation lacing her voice.

"You left your spare here last time because you wanted to have one here at all times," I counter, keeping my voice gentle.

"Damn it, Attie, can't you just let it go?" she snaps, shooting to her feet and glaring at me. "I don't want to get in the damn hot tub. So, stop asking me."

I stare at her in shock as she storms into the house and slams the door behind her. *What the hell just happened?* She has never snapped at me like that before, but in the last twenty-four hours she's done it twice. She's never even raised her voice with me. I don't know who this girl is, but she is not my Rose.

Sighing, I grab the blanket off the swing and go into the cabin. After folding the blanket and sitting it on the back of the couch, I go to the kitchen and wash the mug in the sink. Since we are leaving in a few hours, I don't want to leave anything dirty.

After the kitchen and living rooms are clean, I run down to the theater room and the game room, picking up any loose trash before going up to my room and getting my things together. I stop in the hall and knock on Rosalind's door. "Rose? Can we talk?"

"No. I just want to go home," Rose says through the closed door.

Cursing under my breath, I close my eyes and rest my forehead against the door frame. "Okay, well... if you're ready, we can head out in twenty minutes," I inform her. I know she needs her space to cool off, but damn. I just want to make sure she is okay.

Twenty minutes later, her door creaks open, and her soft footsteps pad down the stairs. Our eyes meet. That genuine smile from earlier is long gone, replaced by her usual detached expression.

"Ready?" I ask, reaching for her bag. My brow furrows when she shrugs away from me and nods.

"Yep. Let's go," she says in a voice so soft I have to strain to hear her.

"Oookay?" I say as I grab my bag off the floor and head out the door behind her. After locking the door and setting the alarm, I throw my bag into the back of the Jeep. When I get in, Rosalind is already buckled in and ready to go, her music playing loud enough that I know she doesn't want to talk. I sigh as I turn it down. "Rosalind. What is going on? Why did you freak out so bad?"

"Nothing. Can we just go home now?" she asks as she locks her phone and places it on her lap.

Nodding, I put the car in reverse and back out of the driveway. This is going to be a long drive.

Chapter Twelve
Rosalind

Fighting with Attie is the last thing I want to be doing right now. If I get any more stressed about things in my life, I am going to lose my mind. I didn't mean to snap at him, but damn, I just wanted him to stop with the hot tub. I know that he's confused. I don't blame him.

Halfway through the drive home, I reach over to grab his hand. Lacing our fingers together, I look over at him. "I'm sorry I snapped at you. Every little thing has been setting me off over the last couple of days. I really am sorry."

He nods. "I'm not going to tell you it's okay, because it isn't, but I am going to acknowledge and accept your apology. Just next time, please try not to snap at me. We should be able to have a conversation without you biting my head off, honey."

Hearing him call me honey sends a shiver through me. Those little pet names are going to be the death of me. I'm going to end up in one big puddle on the floor if he keeps it up. I gently squeeze his hand and nod. "You're right. I will do better."

We spent the rest of the drive in silence, but this time it's not awkward, angry silence. It's a comfortable silence. About twenty minutes away from home, I start bouncing my knee, another one of my anxious traits. Sensing my apprehension, Atticus lets go of my hand and rests his hand on my thigh, rubbing small circles with his thumb. *His touch is like magic*, I think as I feel my anxiety lessening.

Once we arrive at my house, I groan at the sight of my mom's car in the driveway. I was hoping she'd be at work, or really anywhere but here.

"Do you want me to come in?" Atticus asks as he follows my gaze to my mom's car.

"No, it's okay. I'm just going to go to bed anyway," I say, glancing at the clock on the dashboard. It's only six p.m. but by the time I shower and grab something quick for dinner, it will be an acceptable time for me to climb into bed.

"I'll text you later. Trevor and I will grab your car from campus and bring it back this evening." he says as he leans over and kisses me softly. "Have a good night, Rose." Reaching in the back seat, he grabs my overnight bag and sits it in my lap.

"Let me know when you get home. Be careful please," I lean in for another kiss before I hop out of the car and run inside.

Just as I step into the hallway to head up to my room, I hear my mom on the phone in the kitchen. Deciding to get it over with now, I follow her voice. "Hey mom. I'm home." She just nods and goes back to her conversation. I roll my eyes and shuffle through the cabinets, looking for something to eat.

Once I'm satisfied with my snacks, I grab a water and make my way to my room. Sitting the snacks on the bed, I grab my favorite pair of pajamas, silk shorts and a matching long sleeve button up, then run to the bathroom for a quick shower. Checking my phone, I find a few messages from Atticus. One telling me he made it home safely after he and Trevor dropped my car off, and then another telling me he missed me. How cheesy. I love it.

We text back and forth for a few hours before I feel sleep beginning to take over. After saying goodnight and putting my phone on charge, I pull the covers up to my chin, close my eyes, and let myself drift off to sleep.

Unfortunately, sleep doesn't come as easy as it did last night. I jolt awake mid-nightmare and I am thrown into a full-blown panic attack at three-thirty a.m. It's almost like I'm in the dream. I can feel Derek still clutching my throat, stopping me from taking full breaths. His bruising grip on my arms as he held me down. Bile rises in my throat, and I grab my bed side trash can, emptying the contents of my stomach. Tears running down my face, I try to calm my breathing.

I haven't had an attack this severe before. Reluctantly, I grab my phone. Pressing number three on my speed dial, I wait as the line rings. *Please pick up.*

"Rose?" As soon as I hear the groggy voice, more tears begin to fall.

"Atticus...." I whisper, "I need you."

On the other end of the phone, I can hear the jingle of his keys and the door to his house shutting. Once he's in the car, he soothingly says, "I'm already on my way, baby, unlock the balcony door. Do you want me to stay on the phone?"

"Yes please," I whisper as I reach over to unlock the door that is right beside my bed.

"Are you hurt?" he asks, his voice full of worry.

"N-no," I breathe. Just hearing his voice calms my panic ever so slightly. I'm still having a challenging time taking deep breaths, and the nausea is still very present, but at least I don't feel like I'm going to suffocate anymore. "How far away are you?"

"Turning down your street now," he says. His house is a whopping ten minutes from mine, so the fact that he is so close already doesn't faze me. "I'm going to hang up now, but I'm coming up the steps to the balcony," he assures me.

As soon as he hangs up, I hear the doorknob turning. A wave of relief washes over me as he steps inside. "Attie...."

Chapter Thirteen
Atticus

It's three-thirty in the morning when my phone starts ringing. "Who in the hell?" I groan as I roll over and grab it. When I read the screen, concern courses through me. "Rose?" I question, half asleep, just as I'm met with her cries. The sound of her crying is like someone dumping ice water on my head. I'm wide awake and already getting up to throw some clothes on. As soon as she says she needs me, I'm out the door.

"Are you hurt?"

"No." She says, "How far away are you?"

"Turning down your street now," I say. I've never been so thankful for the short drive to her house from mine. I park on the street behind her car and get out. "I'm going to hang up now, but I'm coming up the steps to the balcony," I assure her before hanging up and climbing the steps.

As I open the door, my eyes search the dimly lit room for Rose. They land on her tiny figure, sitting on her bed with her knees pulled up to her chest. When she says my name, I rush over and sit down on her bed, pulling her into my lap. "It's okay. I'm here," I whisper as I kiss the top of her head. She starts crying into my shirt, and I just hold her. I don't speak, in fear that she might pull away and close back down on me. Keeping my lips pressed to the top of her head, I continue to run my hand up and down her back, offering as much comfort as I can.

After several moments pass, I pull back to look into her chocolate brown eyes. My heart breaks as I take in their red and puffy appearance.

"I'm s-sorry I woke you," she breathes out. Her eyes searching mine for any hint of anger. She knows as well as I do that she's not going to find any there, though.

"Rose, you know I don't care about that. What I care about is if you are okay?"

"I-" she begins, but as she shifts, her shorts rise up and something catches my eye. It's like someone has sucked all the oxygen out of the room.

"Rosalind. What the hell is this?" I ask as I take in the cuts on her thighs. "Please... please tell me I'm seeing things," I plead, gently running my thumb across one of the healing cuts. She looks down while chewing on her bottom lip. "Rose..." my voice soft, "is this what you've been hiding from me?" I ask. I don't try to mask the hurt in my voice now. I know that's not what she needs right now, but I'm running on full emotions.

"I didn't want to upset you," she whispers.

"Rosalind," I say. I use my finger to lift her chin, making her look at me. "I can't imagine the pain you are going through, but this isn't the only way to get relief... I just don't understand what is hurting you so much." I search her sad eyes, desperate for some hint of an answer.

"I can't tell you," she mumbles, and I raise my eyebrows.

"Why not, Rose?" I ask, the emotion clear in my voice. I'm hurt. How could she keep this from me? How did I not notice?

"I just can't, okay?" Rosalind said climbing, out of my arms and moving to sit on the edge of the bed.

As she moves, her hair falls back, no longer providing a curtain over her neck and something else grabs my attention. Bruising in the shape of a hand around her neck. The sight alone makes my stomach churn.

"Rosalind. Olivia," I fume, "Who the *fuck* did that to you?"

Rosalind sees the fury in my face and her hand immediately goes to her neck. "Drop it Attie," she pleads.

My jaw drops in disbelief as I move closer to inspect the bruising on her neck. "I absolutely will *not* drop this, Rose." *Is she for real?* Looking at her face, she is serious. There's no way in hell I'm going to just drop this.

"Atticus *stop*!" Rose jumps to her feet, tears falling from her eyes.

"I don't fucking understand, Rosalind. We don't keep secrets from each other, and you can't even trust me enough to tell me who hurt you so badly that you are physically hurting yourself?" I'm trying to hold on to my emotions, but I'm losing it. I'm not even angry with her. I'm more hurt than anything because she kept this secret from me.

After a moment of silence, I drop my head into my hands. "Rose, I just want to make sure that you are safe. I care about you so much, and the fact that someone has hurt you makes my blood boil. I can't help that I'm angry," I say, exasperated. Realization dawns on me as I look over at her. "This is why you didn't want to get in the hot tub this weekend, isn't it?" I question.

When she nods her head, I fist my hands in my lap. "Do you have any other bruises?" I ask.

"My upper arms, and my wrist," she whispers.

I don't know who this person is, but I'm going to kill them.

Chapter Fourteen
Rosalind

As I stand by the edge of the bed, listening to Atticus speak, I can't help but stare at him in shock. "Please Atticus, I really don't need you to be upset with me. I know I just shouted at you, and I'm sorry. I'm really struggling right now." My voice is so low, Atticus has to lean closer to me to hear. "I don't want to keep this from you. But if I tell you, I'm afraid of what will happen."

"What do you mean, you're afraid of what would happen?" Atticus says, confusion written on his face. I don't miss the fact that he has my sheets gripped so tightly in his hands that his knuckles are white.

"I'm afraid of what will happen to you. If I tell you, your basketball career is going to suffer. I didn't want you to find out about this," I gesture to my leg, "because I didn't want you to feel guilty for not noticing. Everything I've kept from you is because I didn't want any negative repercussions for you."

"Rose, you didn't tell me that someone assaulted you and that you were hurting yourself to protect me?" He asks, the frustration clear in his voice.

No matter how much I fight it, my tears finally fall. "He said he would ruin us both. I'm a nobody, so it wouldn't affect me as much, but you, you have so much to lose, Atticus." I tip my head back, looking up at the ceiling before closing my eyes briefly.

"Hold on. Who is 'he'? What do you mean he said he would ruin me?" he grits out, anger lacing his words.

Sighing, I reopen my eyes and look down at my hands. There's no getting around this. "Last week, I was studying in the library before the game, and I hadn't moved my car…" I begin, keeping my eyes down on my fingers as I pick at the skin. "After the scrimmage, when I was walking past the science and arts buildings, I was pulled into the alley between them." My hands begin to shake as I recall the events of that night.

"He had asked me out that same day, and I turned him down. He had been asking me out for a few weeks, a couple times when he came to class with lingering effects from his latest party, and I turned him down every time. But boy, was he persistent. He usually took it pretty good, only getting angry the last two or three times that I rejected him… this time, though, it was different. He grabbed my arm and drug me into the alley between the two buildings." I keep my eyes on my shaking hands, because if I look at Atticus, I will break.

"He pushed me up against the wall and told me to stop playing hard to get. One hand was wrapped around my throat and the other…" I stop. Looking up at him, seeing the pure rage in his features, I can't stop the sobs that escape me. "I tried to scream, but the grip he had on my neck was so tight. I begged him to stop and even told him I would go out with him if he just let me go. Finally, someone got close enough to spook him off. Even though they were still far enough away, we just looked like a couple of kids fooling around."

"Who was it, Rose?" Atticus asks, attempting to keep his voice steady.

"It was Derek Murphy," I say before looking up at him. "He threatened to destroy you and me if I ever told anyone. I didn't want to do that to you, and I was ashamed. So, I kept quiet."

He grabbed my hand and pulled me onto his lap again. "Oh, Rose… I'm so sorry, baby." As his eyes filled with tears, he whispered, "I'm so sorry." I know that it's hurting him to hear this. I would feel the same way if the roles were reversed. "I should have skipped the shower and walked you to your car. If I would've known..." he trails off, glancing away and then back at me. "I'm going to kill him."

"That is exactly why I didn't tell you. Please promise me that you won't do anything stupid, Attie," I say, exasperated.

"*Seriously?* You're asking me to just ignore this?" he asks incredulously.

"I know you don't understand..." I mumble.

"You're absolutely right. I don't understand, Rosalind. Someone *hurt* you and you are hurting yourself and you want me to just let it go?" His voice starting to raise again, and I shrink back slightly. He notices my reaction and regret flashes across his face.

"Atticus..." I start, "It's not going to make a difference. His family is one of the top donors to the university. No one will believe me. All it will do is hurt you and I both."

"It's already hurt you Rose, and it's continuing to hurt you," he says, lowering his tone as he looks down at the cuts on my legs, "and if it's hurting you... it's hurting me. I don't give a shit what happens to me. What I care about is Derek getting what he deserves."

Sighing, I move out of his lap and stand. "This was a mistake. I shouldn't have told you. You're going to do the complete opposite of what I asked and go after him anyway," I snap, unable to hide the irritation in my voice. Looking at the clock, I see that it's almost five a.m. Slipping on that perfect, 'everything is fine' mask that I've worn far too long, I square my shoulders and turn back to him. "I'm feeling much better. You should go. You have practice in an hour."

"Rose, I'm not leav-" he starts, but I hold my hand up to stop him.

"I don't want to hear it. I will be fine. I need you to leave," I say as I walk over to the balcony door. "Promise me that you won't confront Derek this morning," I plead.

"You and I both know I don't make promises I can't keep," he says before kissing the top of my head. "I will be back after practice. We aren't done talking about this."

After he's gone, I lay down on the bed and stare up at the ceiling. I shouldn't have told him. I know that he isn't going to be able to keep a handle on his emotions and will end up in trouble.

Derek is going to ruin him, and I will be responsible.

Chapter Fifteen

Atticus

When I get to the Jeep, my mind is reeling. Earlier when I got to Rose's, I didn't expect either bomb to be dropped on me. How the fuck do I keep missing the signs that the people in my life are hurting? First Kayla, my sister, tried to kill herself after our parents died. Now Rose, the love of my life, is hurting herself.

I meant what I said when I told Rose I didn't make promises I couldn't keep. Derek's family may be top donors, and it may cost me my spot on the team, but I would do anything to ensure Rose is safe from that piece of shit.

Looking at the clock, I put the car in drive. If I don't get a move on, I will be late, and it won't help my case when Derek gets what I have planned for him. Driving to the gym, I run through everything that Rose told me. I hardly ever cry. Let alone allow someone else to see me cry. But damn it, I was close to breaking down in front of her. I can't imagine all the shit she has been dealing with because of what Derek did to her.

When I get to the gym, I grab my practice bag I keep in the car and head inside. I'm one of the last ones to arrive, but at this moment, that's the last thing on my mind. Turning the corner of one set of lockers, I hear Derek laughing. The sound makes my blood boil. Before I know it, I'm rounding the last set coming face to face with him.

"Yo man, you're later than usual," he says as he reaches out to fist bump me, his usual greeting and I glare down at him. He's just a few inches shorter than me, even though we are evenly matched for muscle tone "Did you finally get a shot at that wildfire?" he teases. He doesn't know it yet, but mentioning Rose was the absolute worst thing he could've done right now.

The next couple of seconds pass in a blur. I grab him by his throat and slam him up against the locker. "Atticus... what the hell, man? Let me go," he strains out.

"How's it feel, hmm? How does it feel to have someone hold you by your throat and not let you go?" I ask, keeping my voice low so that only he can hear it. Our teammates are starting to crowd around us, completely shocked at the sight before them. I am usually more reserved and having an outburst like this is unlike me.

I tighten my grip on his throat before I lean in closer. "If you so much as look in Rose's direction again, I will not hesitate to knock you the fuck out. I don't give a damn who your parents are. Do you understand?"

Recognition flashes in his eyes as he hears the reason behind my rage. "So, the bitch told you," he says with a smirk. Just as I'm about to open my mouth to reply, Coach comes in.

"What the hell is going on here?" he booms.

"Nothing Coach, just making sure Derek here is on the same page as me," I say as I push against Derek's throat before releasing him.

"Save that for outside the gym. We don't need that shit this season," Coach grumbles before adding, "Get your asses out on the court. Now."

Practice goes by agonizingly slow. I didn't want to leave Rose like I did. She's upset with me, and to be honest, I'm upset with myself. The signs were all there. The clothing, avoiding the hot tub at the cabin, the interactions with Derek I've witnessed since then. I just didn't put them together. But never in a million years did I imagine that Rosalind would be hurting herself.

Derek and I take jabs at each other all throughout practice. I get an elbow to the face. He gets a knee to the groin, and many other things.

Toward the end, I get a fast break and go for a layup. Right as I go to lay it in the basket, I'm hit from the side. It knocks me off balance and I stumble into the goal post, hitting my shoulder hard.

"What the hell?" Turning to face the guy that ran into me. I'm not surprised to see Derek standing a few feet away with the tiniest hint of a smirk. "That was a cheap shot, and you know it," I shout as I close the distance between us.

"I'm completely innocent," Derek says as he shrugs. "Coach didn't blow the whistle, so it's a fair play."

"Fair play my ass," I mumble before pushing him out of my face. I'm so consumed with rage that I barely notice Trevor trying to insert himself between the two of us.

"Hey man," Trevor says, pushing me away from Derek. "Come on, it's not worth it," he says.

"Get out of my way, Trevor," I say, glaring down at him.

Just as I go to step around him, Coach blows his whistle. "I don't know what has gotten into you, Reed. But I want you off my court," he bellows.

"It's not just me," I protest, but it's no use. I may be the star player, but Derek is the golden boy.

To get to the locker room, I have to pass Derek. His smug face makes the anger boil over. Before I have time to think about the consequences of my next move, I stop in front of him and swing. As my fist makes contact, the sound of his nose crunching rings out.

"What the *fuck*," Derek yells.

"*Reed*. That's it. Two game suspension," Coach yells.

I should be pissed, but I don't care. The smugness that was previously on Derek's face is now replaced with shock. I shove my way past him and the crowd that gathered around us.

Anxious to get back to Rose, I forego my shower, deciding to shower at her house. Grabbing my bag, I rush out to my Jeep. After typing out a quick text to Rose asking if she's hungry, I make my way to pick up my favorite after practice meal.

As I pull up to the quaint little taco truck, my phone dings with Rose's reply.

Starving, grab me a three pack.

I chuckle to myself as I walk up to the window and place my order. One thing I love about this truck is that it never takes long for your food to be done. I'm back in my jeep and on my way to Rose's house within ten minutes.

When I arrive, I grab the food bags from the passenger seat and make my way up the steps to her balcony. Knocking twice, I shift the food in my hand just as Rose opens the door. Seeing the food, her mouth turns up, giving way to the slightest hint of a smile.

It quickly disappears when she looks from the tacos to my face. With a gasp, she reaches up and brushes a piece of hair away from my eye. "What happened to your face?" Until this moment, I had completely forgotten about Derek elbowing me in the face.

"It's nothing. I just took an elbow to the face." I explain with a shrug.

Rose studies me as if trying to decipher my lie. "Right, so that's why your hand is messed up as well."

Damn, nothing gets by this woman. Unable to keep lying to her, I sit the food on her nightstand and sit on the bed. "Alright... I may or may not have punched Derek in the face after I told him to stay away from you," I say with a sigh. Avoiding her glare, I look down at my hand, smirking as I remember the look on his face after I punched him.

"Atticus Michael Reed," Rose grinds out. "I told you to leave it alone. Why can't you listen?"

"I can't leave it alone, Rose. I need you to understand that someone hurt you, the woman I love, and I am not about to sit by and let it slide."

I cross my arms over my chest, leaning back against the headboard. "I didn't do anything he didn't deserve."

"Yeah, and now there will be consequences to your actions," she mumbles. "You might think you're doing me a great service by getting into altercations with Derek, but really, you're just hurting me."

Her words are like daggers to my soul. I never wanted to hurt her. In fact, I only want the best for her. Is she right? Have I just hurt her more?

Chapter Sixteen

Rosalind

Atticus just confessed his love for me, and I can't even touch on that fact because I'm so angry. I asked him to leave the Derek thing alone, but he couldn't. Now we will both have to deal with the fallout.

"Rose. I will be fine. I got suspended for two games, so what?" Atticus says with a shrug.

"You got *suspended*?" I sit down at the foot of the bed and start picking at the skin around my nails. *He got suspended because of me. It's already started. What next? What's Derek going to do to me?* I'm getting restless. My thoughts are clouded with worry as my knee starts to bounce.

"Baby," Atticus says, moving closer to me. "Look at me," he whispers, resting his hand on my thigh. Reluctantly, I lift my head to look at him.

"I'm ruining your life, Atticus." I can't stop the tears that begin to fall.

"You are most certainly not ruining my life," he states firmly. "Don't ever think that. I made the conscious decision to punch him. I will deal with the repercussions. I don't regret it at all."

I chew on my bottom lip as I let his words sink in. "I just don't want you to suffer because of me," I whisper.

Atticus wraps his arms around me, squeezing gently. "Don't worry about me. I can take whatever that asshole throws at me," he assures me.

Nodding, I lean back into him. Even with his arms around me, I can't fight the dread that has formed in my stomach. My mind is racing as I think of the potential repercussions of his outburst. Derek comes from old money and his parents contribute a significant amount of funds to the college. Especially to the basketball program. Even if I filed a report, they would sweep it under the rug. No one wants to piss off their biggest donors.

Sensing my apprehension, Atticus gives me a firm hug, holding tightly for a moment. Confused, I look over my shoulder at him. "What was that for?" I ask. The anxiety I'm feeling begins to dissipate slowly.

"When you were sleeping yesterday morning, I was doing research on how to help you through your anxiety attacks," he says sheepishly. "An article said that giving a firm hug as a form of deep pressure therapy, can activate your parasympathetic nervous system. Which in turn helps lessen your anxiety because of the calming effect."

Looking at him, I'm completely shocked. Although, I'm not sure why, because Atticus always looks for ways to help people. "You did that for me?" I ask softly.

"Rosalind, I would do anything to make you happy. That includes finding ways to help you cope when everything gets too much," he states as he brushes the hair out of my face before pressing a soft kiss to my forehead.

Unable to find the words to show my appreciation for his thoughtfulness, I give him a grateful smile as I squeeze his hand. How on earth did I get lucky enough to have someone like Atticus in my life? I'll never know, but I will forever be thankful.

The next few days pass without incident. Atticus and I spend even more time together, whether it's him spending the night at my house or vice versa. Since he's suspended, per the team's code of conduct, he isn't allowed to practice either. So, we spend our days cuddled up, watching movies, and eating as much junk food as our bodies can handle. Neither of us brings up Derek or the self-harm, content in our own little bubble. Unfortunately for us, the bubble never lasts.

Chapter Seventeen

Atticus

My phone's incessant notifications have me waking with a groan. *What the hell is going on?* Rolling over, careful not to wake Rose, I grab my phone. *Shit.* There are several missed calls and messages from Trevor. The one that makes me sit straight up, though, is from Coach asking me to come into his office before practice this morning. I'm still suspended, so I'm confused. But as I reread the message, I have a nagging feeling this is not good.

Looking over at the clock, dread fills my stomach. I need to be there in less than half an hour. Rose is still peacefully sleeping beside me, and I wish I could stay with her. She has been sleeping better since I have spent every night with her since her panic attack. But I know this meeting with Coach is important, so after a quick kiss to her head, I reluctantly climb out of bed.

Throwing on some sweats and a hoodie before walking back to the bed, I lean down and gently wake Rose just enough so she can comprehend what I'm saying. "Hey babe, I have to run to the gym for a meeting. I promise I will be right back." I brush the hair from her face before leaning down and placing a soft kiss on her lips.

She sleepily mumbles goodbye, and I chuckle. She is adorable. Grabbing my phone and my keys, I make my way to my Jeep. The drive to the gym feels like it takes forever. The apprehension heavy in my stomach as

I pull into my parking spot. Coincidentally, Trevor arrives at the same time. He's always early so it shouldn't surprise me.

"Hey man," he says as he jogs over to me once out of the car, "I have tried to call you all morning."

"Yeah sorry. I have been sleeping like a rock since Rose has been staying with me." I tell him. "Do you know what's going on? Why does Coach want a meeting with me?"

"Well, that's what I was calling you about. Apparently, Derek's parents have been on the school's ass about doing something about the fact that you punched their precious spawn of Satan and broke his nose." Hearing Derek's parents are involved now makes me groan. "Which was great, by the way. I give it a solid ten."

I smirk as I remember the look on his face. Stopping in front of Coach's office, I turn to look at Trevor. "This is going to be a nightmare," I say before I nod to him and head inside. Coach is sitting at his large mahogany desk. He may look small, but he is intimidating. The saying 'his bark is worse than his bite' is not applicable to him.

"Morning Reed," he mumbles as he looks up from his stack of papers. "I'm sure you're wondering why I called you here when you aren't even practicing," he begins. Not one to beat around the bush, he always gets straight to the point. "Derek's parents have demanded that I throw you off the team... well, actually, they want you kicked out of school, but I don't have authority over that. They've started an investigation with the school board." *An investigation? Fuck.* I shift uncomfortably in my seat. This whole conversation is making me nervous.

Not waiting for me to reply, he continues, "I don't want to throw you off the team. You're our star player and your absence is hurting us. I'm sure you have good reasons for your actions, but I can't condone them." Sighing, I hang my head. I know where this is going. "I need your gear turned in by the end of the day."

I could contest his decision, but I know it will only make things worse. I nod before standing. "I'll be back with my stuff soon," I say before going toward the locker room.

As I'm gathering my things from my locker and stuffing them into my team bag, I hear a voice that makes my blood pressure rise instantly. Derek. Acting on the urge to punch him again wouldn't help my case, so I grit my teeth and jerk my bag off the bench.

There's no avoiding him, because to get to Coach's office, I have to go through the back of the locker room. Keeping my head down, I grip the strap of my bag tightly. I push past one of his friends who shoulder checks me. Derek laughs, and I raise my eyes to glare at him. "Nice face," I muse.

"I see Coach gave you the great news." He gestures to my bag.

"It's hardly fair when mommy and daddy bail you out of everything," I spit back. *Only a few more feet to the door. Keep it together, you're almost out,* I tell myself.

"Have fun with your whore," he calls out. I don't even have a chance to drop my bag before Trevor is already on him.

"What the hell did you just say?" Trevor grits out, grabbing Derek by the shirt and throwing him up against the locker. Rose may be my girlfriend, but our friend group is close knit, and she is like a sister to him. I would react the same way if it were Amelia he was talking about.

"What? I'm only speaking the truth. She practically threw herself at me after the scrimmage," Derek says with a smirk.

As the words leave his mouth, I put my hand on Trevor's arm, pulling him out of the way. Derek doesn't have time to react before I pull back and slam my fist into his face with enough force that it bounces his head off the locker. His friends protest, but none of them step in. I'm seeing red as I get two more hits in. If I could, I would hit him for every single mark on Rose's body. Even then, it wouldn't be enough.

"*Reed*," Coach bellows from his doorway. "Get off of him!"

Trevor is now pulling at me. Not wanting to make things worse, I drop Derek and turn to Coach.

"My office. *Now*." I take in a deep breath and exhale before picking up my bag and following him into the office.

"Reed. You have just screwed yourself out of any chance you had of coming back to this team," he says with an exasperated sigh. "I don't know what's going on between you two, but I hope it was worth it," he adds before reaching for my bag.

Handing my basketball gear over, I turn on my heel to leave. "Coach, it's worth everything and more," I say, opening the door and pausing. "And I'd do it again in a heartbeat," I add before leaving. The locker room is quiet as I walk through. Not even Trevor says anything as I pass him, but he raises his eyebrows and purses his lips together in his signature 'we'll talk later' look.

Once in the car, I sit there in silence. Basketball has been my life since I was 5 years old. As soon as I was able to play on one of those little peewee teams, I fell in love with the game. Now, I've lost it all. I grip the steering wheel, staring at my bloody knuckles. Rose is going to kill me.

Fuck. What am I going to do now?

Chapter Eighteen

Rosalind

I'm standing in the kitchen when I hear Atticus's keys unlocking the door. Placing my cup of coffee down on the counter, I walk into the living room. "Hey honey, where have you-" I stop short, seeing the look on his face. "Attie... what's wrong?"

"Rose, I'm sorry," he whispers.

Confused, I walk closer to him. "What happened?" I ask again, placing my hands on his shoulders. "Are you okay?"

Atticus sighs before placing his hands on mine, squeezing softly. "Come sit down," he says gently.

I freeze as I take in the sight of his bloody knuckles. My hands slide from his shoulders and drop to my sides. "Please tell me you didn't get into another fight, Atticus..."

"Just please come sit down," he whispers before leading me over to the couch and sitting down.

Gently taking his hand in mine, I inspect the injuries. "Atticus, you're worrying me."

"Derek's parents had me kicked off the team today." His words cause me to drop his hand. Oh, my god. What have I done?

"No. No, they can't do that," I rush out. "You don't deserve it."

"I do deserve it though, Rose." My eyes are filling with tears as I look at him. "I attacked him, not just once, but twice," he says before reaching for my hand.

"What do you mean twice? Is that what happened to your hands? Atticus, I *told* you to leave it alone," I say as I pull my hand back. "You love basketball. It is everything to you. Why did you have to do this?" I ask, tears running down my face. I am furious with him.

Atticus gently grabs my shoulders and looks me in the eye. "Rose, yes, I love basketball, but it isn't everything to me. Not anymore," he whispers.

Looking away from him, I chew on my bottom lip. This is all my fault. "I never should have told you. I wish I hadn't called you that night," I whisper shakily. It's only partly true. If it wasn't for him coming to my rescue, I don't know how long the panic attack would have gone on. I know my words hurt him. I can tell by the way he shifts away from me.

"Well, I'm glad you did Rose. You don't have to suffer alone," he says softly.

"I was doing just fine," I snap, and he scoffs. "What's that for?" I ask, turning to look at him.

"You and I both know that's a lie," he snaps back at me before quickly standing. "If you were doing fine, then you wouldn't be hurting yourself, Rosalind."

"I'm just going to go home," I say as I stand and walk in the opposite direction toward the bedroom. I hear his footsteps behind me as I grab my overnight bag I've been living out of the last two nights. "Don't even try to stop me right now, Atticus."

"Heaven forbid, I try to help you," he mumbles, going to sit on his bed. "I just wish you'd stop pushing me away."

Wiping the tears from my face, I turn to look at him. "I shouldn't have even let you get this close to begin with." I say before leaving. I don't know if it was the shock of what I just said or if he just didn't care, but I manage to make it to my car and out of the driveway without him trying to stop me.

I make the ten-minute drive home in five. Sitting in the silence, I begin to process everything that had just happened. The things I said to Atticus were hurtful. I didn't mean them, and I think deep down he knows that. But I can't handle being responsible for him losing his spot on the team.

Shutting my car off, I get out and go inside. I don't even bother to check if mom is home. It's not like she would care about anything that's happening to me. Once I get into my bedroom, I throw my bag on the bed and head to the bathroom. I need to feel something other than this aching in my chest.

Half an hour later, I emerge from the shower. After bandaging a wound on my leg that was accidentally worse than intended, I put on sweatpants and a t-shirt. As I climb into bed, I grab my phone. I have several missed calls and messages from Atticus. The last one, though, makes my heart break.

I love you, Rose.

I can't respond. I have just done the one thing I promised him I wouldn't do, and I feel like shit. He is going to hate me if he finds out. I reach into my nightstand and grab the melatonin. If I'm sleeping alone tonight, I will need it. Once I take it, I turn on my side and curl up under the covers. The combination of melatonin and pure exhaustion from crying most of the day has me slipping into sleep much faster than usual.

🌹

The next week is a blur. The nightmares are back, and I am sleeping less and less. Atticus texts me every morning and every night, reminding me that he loves me. I usually just reply with one-word answers, enough so that he doesn't worry. I know he means well, but I just can't bring myself to face him right now.

It's the day before classes start back and I am sitting on the couch watching TV when there's a knock at the door. Part of me hopes that Atticus has come to bring me to my senses.

"Attie, I don't want to talk-" I say as I open the door, but to my surprise it's not Atticus, but instead a very pissed off Amelia.

"Rosalind Olivia Johnson," she fumes. "Can you tell me why I have a very worried Atticus calling me and asking me to make a house call?" Pushing her way past me, she shoots me a glare.

I sigh as I step aside. Of course, he called Amelia.

"So," she begins as she sits down on the couch and crosses her legs, "What is going on? You've been ignoring my calls all week too, so save your 'it's nothing' bullshit for someone else."

"Amelia. I'm fine. I don't even know why he called you," I say, sitting across from her and avoiding her eyes.

"Yeah... and that's why you look like shit, right?" she says and tilts her head to the side with a raised eyebrow. Damn, it's been a while since I've been on Amelia's tough love side. I had almost forgotten what it felt like.

"I got him kicked off the team," I whisper, looking down at my hands.

"What do you mean, Rose? Trevor said he got kicked off for fighting with Derek. Twice. Nothing about you," she says as she uncrosses her legs and leans forward, resting her elbows on her knees.

"I'm the reason he got into the fight with Derek," I say before looking up at her with tears in my eyes. "It's my fault," I repeat.

Seeing the pain on my face, Amelia abandons her spot and comes to join me. Sitting beside me, she reaches over and grabs my hand. "From what I understand, whatever they were fighting over was worth Derek getting knocked down a notch or two," she says before squeezing my hand gently. "Trevor also got involved. But he didn't get a hit in. Atticus stopped him." Amelia sighs. "Why can't you tell me what happened? Did you really come onto Derek like he's telling people? Is that why Atticus is upset?" she asks.

"He's telling people that?" I ask, "How long has he been spreading those lies?"

"It started the day after the scrimmage," she replies, contemplating her next words. "What happened?" she asks again.

Dropping my head into my hands, I let out a groan. "If I tell you, will you promise me that you won't tell a soul? No matter what I say, and no matter how upset you get?"

Eyeing me warily, Amelia nods. "You're my best friend, Rose. I'm not going to tell anyone anything you don't want me to," she promises.

I nod before scooting back on the couch so I can cross my legs. "Okay, so it was the night of the scrimmage…" I start. As I tell her about the incident, anger and sorrow cross over her face. I tell her everything, about what he did and the threats that followed. Well, almost everything, I don't dare mention the cutting. Once I finish, there are tears in her eyes.

"I don't know what to say, Rose," she starts, and I shake my head, but she places her hand on mine before continuing, "But I do know that you have an endless amount of support through our friend group. Trevor, Atticus, and I will always be in your corner." Then she leans over and wraps her arms around me, holding me.

"I don't know how to face Atticus. I hate myself for being the reason he has to give up the biggest part of his life," I mutter into her shoulder.

Amelia pulls back from the hug and wipes the tears from her face. "Rose, listen to me." She grabs my hands again. "Sometimes in life, you have to change paths. You figure out what's more important, something that's only in your life for a season, or something that you want for the rest of your life. Atticus made his choice. Trevor told me that when Coach told him he hoped whatever caused this was worth it, Atticus said, and I quote, 'it was worth everything and more, and I'd do it again in a heartbeat.'"

Speechless, I put a hand over my mouth, stifling a gasp. "I don't- I don't know what to say," I whisper.

"How about you don't say anything and go to Atticus? It's clear that you both need to be with each other right now. Trevor says he's been a wreck since you left the other night," she adds as she stands, pulling me up with her.

Nodding, I grab my phone and keys off the table before I turn to Amelia. "Thank you," I say, giving her a hug. "Thank you for being such a great friend, and for listening to me."

"That's what I'm here for, Rose, now go," she says, shooing me out the door.

I make it to Atticus's house in record timing. Sitting in his driveway, I give myself a pep talk. "He loves you, Rose. He doesn't hate you," I repeat as I climb out of the car and walk to the front door. As I reach up to knock on the door, it swings open and all the fears I had dissipate immediately.

Chapter Nineteen
Atticus

She's on her way.

I reread the message three times before I jump up from the couch. She's coming back. Is it to yell at me for pushing Amelia on her, or is she coming back for good? While I hope it's the latter of the two, I just want to see her.

Hearing her car door shut, I run to the front door and swing it open just as she's about to knock. As we stand there looking at each other, I take in her appearance. I frown as I notice the dark circles under her eyes. They had taken so long to go away before, and now they're back.

It's clear neither of us is going to move, so I take a step toward her and when she doesn't flinch away, I take it as an invitation to wrap my arms around her. Pulling her close to me, I lay my head on top of hers and breathe in the familiar scent of her coconut shampoo. The last week without her has been torture. I have barely slept because I have been so worried. But I knew that she needed space, so I tried my damndest to respect her wishes.

"Attie," Rose breathes out against my chest as her arms go around my waist.

"I missed you so fucking much, baby," I whisper.

"I missed you, too." She pulls away to look up at me with tears in her eyes. Reaching up, I wipe away a stray tear from her cheek.

Pulling her inside, I shut the door behind us. Rose gives me a small smile, and all I want at that moment is to kiss those soft lips. I pick her up and carry her into the living room, sitting down on the couch. As soon as her arms wrap around my neck and pull me closer, I can't hold myself back.

When our lips meet, it's like our first kiss all over again. Except this time there's no nervousness between us. Deepening the kiss, I cradle the back of her head. After a few moments, I pull away and rest my forehead against hers. Closing my eyes, I soak in the familiar feeling of her in my arms.

"I love you, Attie," Rose says as she strokes my cheek.

"I love you too, Rose," I say back before kissing her forehead.

"I'm sorry," she whispers. "I'm sorry. I'm the reason you got kicked off the team. I'm sorry for the words I said afterward. I didn't mean them. I'm sorry for ghosting you. Most importantly, I'm sorry for letting you down."

"Letting me down?" I repeat, unsure of what she means. There's nothing she could do to let me down. I wrack my brain to try to decipher what she means, then it hits me like a truck. She must see the moment it clicks in my head, because she quickly drops her head.

"Baby..." I whisper and cup her face, "Can I see them?" I ask softly. She looks at me, confused, before nodding her head and sliding off my lap. She takes a shaky breath before she grabs the top of her sweatpants and slides them down. I slide off the couch and drop to my knees in front of her, taking in each of the fresh new cuts. One is healing slower than the rest, and I notice that it's because it was deeper than the others. Leaning forward, I kiss softly over each cut before sliding her pants back over them.

I look up at her, and the look on her face is full of remorse. Shifting my position slightly, I sit back down on the couch and pull her down into my lap. "You are still the most beautiful girl," I say as I place my finger under her chin. "I'm not going to yell at you. I think you have beaten yourself up enough for doing it. I do wish that you would talk to someone. A professional."

"A therapist?" she questions, nervously chewing on her lip. "Attie, I don't think that's a good idea."

"I'm not making you go. I'm simply asking that you consider it," I assure her.

"I will think about it," Rose promises before leaning in to press her lips to mine.

Nodding, I hug her tightly. "Please don't leave me like that again." I murmur in her ear before burying my face in her neck. Just having her here calms me. I was going out of my mind when she was gone. Trevor finally came over last night and told me I needed to get it together because Rose needed me. I didn't go into details, but after Rose left last week, I called him. He knows that something happened between her and Derek, just not the full story. Which is why I resorted to Amelia. I knew she would be able to get through to Rose.

I'm not sure how long we sit on the couch just holding each other, but my stomach growls loudly, letting me know it's been too long. "You hungry?" I ask softly, looking down into her big brown eyes. With a nod, she pecks my lips and climbs off my lap. Standing up and stretching my arms above my head, I lean back a little, cracking my back.

"Ahh," I say with a sigh of relief, turning to look at Rose. "What do you want to eat?"

"I'm in the mood for spaghetti," she says, walking into the kitchen.

"Spaghetti it is!" I say as I go over to the pantry, pulling out the ingredients.

After twenty minutes we are sitting at the island, eating dinner in comfortable silence. Taking a bite of my spaghetti, I look up at Rose. "Are you staying the night?" I ask sheepishly. I don't want to push her too far because I just got her back, but damn, I need her back in my bed. We both will sleep so much better.

"Umm." Pushing some spaghetti around on her plate, she doesn't look at me when she speaks. "If it's okay with you?" she questions softly. "The nightmares are back..." she trails off as she sits her fork down on her plate.

"Are you kidding me?" I ask. I'm almost certain you can hear the excitement in my voice. "Rose, you have a place in my bed for as long as you want it. It's where you belong," I add and give her a small smile as the relief washes over her features.

Once we finish eating, I wash the dishes while she puts them away. I missed this. I missed her. This last week was the longest I have gone without seeing her in the two years we have been friends.

We head to my bedroom, where I hand her a pair of boxers and one of my t-shirts, before taking her in the bathroom and turning on the bathtub. "Be right back," I say before running to the spare bathroom and grabbing the bubble bath Kayla left when she visited last. Coming back into the bathroom, I pour some into the warm water.

"Attie, you don't have to do this," she says, looking from me to the tub.

"Please baby, just let me take care of you tonight. Tomorrow we go back to classes and I just want to spoil you tonight." I say before taking the hem of her shirt in my hands, waiting for her permission. "If you want me to leave, I will. I won't be upset." I assure her.

"I-I can't," her voice breaks as she steps back.

"Hey, it's okay," I tell her, cupping her face in my hands. "I love you," I add, before leaning down and kissing her gently. "I will be in my room if you need me." I promise.

She nods and I leave the bathroom, giving her privacy. After changing into a pair of pajama pants, I lay down in the bed and scroll through my phone, waiting for her to finish. Half an hour later, I hear the tub draining. Not long after that, the door opens, and she emerges from the bathroom. *Damn, does she look good in my clothes or what?* She's got a towel across her arms in front of her, and it hangs down past her thighs. It's the perfect position for it to hide the scars on her legs.

"Did you enjoy your bath?" I question as I sit up.

She nods and gives me a shy smile. "I did. Thank you."

"Come, lay with me," I say as I flip the covers back for her to climb in.

She walks over and drops the towel before she slides in beside me. "Thank you for not pushing me earlier," she whispers, so faintly I have to strain to hear it.

"Honey, I will never do something without your consent. If you're uncomfortable, that's all you have to say," I tell her before I lay back down and wrap my arms around her tiny frame. "Thank you for coming back."

"I'm not leaving again," she promises.

As we drift off to sleep, I find myself pulling her closer, afraid she's going to disappear again. I know tomorrow is going to be hard for her because she will have to face Derek. Eventually, sleep takes over and stops my worry.

For now.

Chapter Twenty

Rosalind

My heart is racing as I try to catch my breath. I've been running for what seems like miles, but suddenly I'm back in the alley. No. This isn't happening again. But as I look around, I notice things are different. My hands are shaking when my eyes land on Derek's. No. He's in front of me now. His malicious stare causes my stomach to churn.

"Hello, little Rose," he says as he reaches out for my throat, "I told you to keep your mouth shut," he adds.

"No, please," I cry out, trying to grab his hands. "Atticus!" It's useless to call out for him. This alley seems to stretch for miles on either side, and Derek and I are the only two here.

"Your little boyfriend isn't here." His smile is sinister as his grip on my throat tightens.

"No!" I scream, gasping for air. I can't breathe. Tears are running down my face, and I'm thrashing under the covers. Grabbing at my throat, I still can't breathe and I'm panicking.

Hearing my name being repeated over and over in a voice that is not Derek's starts to pull me out of the haze. My chest is still heaving from not being able to breathe, and I feel like I could puke. Now fully aware of my surroundings, I turn to see a terrified Atticus.

"Baby..." he whispers, reaching out for me, but I flinch away.

"Pl-please don't touch me right now," I say, still trying to catch my breath.

He drops his hand to his lap, and the concern on his face grows. I run a shaky hand through my hair while glancing around the room, as if checking to make sure Derek isn't here. Atticus must realize what I'm doing before he speaks again, softly, "It's just us here, honey. You're safe." He promises.

Wiping away the tears on my face, I nod. Unable to sit still, I climb out of bed and start pacing back and forth. Shivering, I rub my hands up and down my arms. "It's okay. You're safe. You're safe." I repeat to myself as I try to shake the feeling of Derek's hand on my throat. The bile in my stomach threatens to come up and I rush to the bathroom, barely making it to the toilet.

Atticus is right behind me, making sure to maintain a distance I'm comfortable with, but close enough I'm aware he's here. We sit in the bathroom in complete silence while I try to calm my breathing and my shaky hands. Fifteen minutes later, I'm no longer struggling to breathe, and I don't feel as anxious.

I look up at Atticus, who is still staring at me, worry covering his face. "I don't want to ask if you're okay, because that was a lot and you obviously aren't," he says before adding, "but are you okay?"

"I've had plenty of nightmares, but none of them have been that real," I say, not wanting to go into detail in fear that it may throw me into another panic attack.

"Can I hold you now?" he asks softly. As soon as I nod, he is beside me and pulling me in his lap. He buries his face in my hair and exhales. My body tenses when he touches me and pulls me close, but I take a deep breath and remind myself that this is Atticus, and he won't hurt me. Relaxing into his touch, I let out a shaky breath.

"I think…" I say and then clear my throat. "That I'm going to see someone…" I trail off, looking at him. "I can't live like this," I whisper.

"I think that is a good idea, baby," he says before leaning down and kissing me on the forehead.

"I don't understand what happened. I usually have no nightmares when I'm with you," I say with a tired sigh.

"Well, we do go back to classes tomorrow…" he points out.

I wring my hands together nervously, "That's true. I'm also stressed because this semester I don't know what classes I have with him and what ones I don't."

"Don't worry, baby. Amelia, Trevor, and I have your back. Okay?" he promises as he places his hands over mine.

I give him a small smile, and then groan. His alarm is going off in the bedroom. It's time to face my fears. Getting up, we head to the bedroom to get ready. As we get in the car, my mind is racing with all the possibilities of what could go wrong today. I can only hope that I don't have many classes with him, or any if I can help it.

Every. Fucking. Class. How can I be so lucky that we have every single class together?

Trevor was able to get one of the guys on the team to tell him what Derek's schedule was, using the excuse that Atticus needed to avoid him as much as possible.

"Maybe you can switch out of your twelve o'clock class?" Atticus suggests, but it's not hopeful.

"I can't… it's a mandatory requisite for my degree." I'm already feeling nervous due to the nightmare this morning, and now I must face being alone with him. I don't know if I can handle it.

Sensing my unease, Atticus reaches over and grabs my hand, lacing our fingers together before he traces tiny circles on the back with his thumb. I know he's trying to calm me, but it's not working.

"We will figure it out. I can transfer in. You won't be alone." Atticus offers.

"I appreciate that. I do," I say, giving him a sad smile. "But you can't do that. You haven't had the pre-requisites, and they won't let you in."

We pull into the parking lot, and the knots in my stomach tighten. "I'm going to throw up," I mumble, leaning my head back against the headrest. My chest is getting heavy, and my breathing is becoming more rapid. I close my eyes and squeeze Atticus's hand, trying to slow my breathing down. Once he's parked, he jumps out of the vehicle and runs over to my side.

Unbuckling, I turn to face him as he opens the door. He pulls me to the edge of the seat, and I bend forward, resting my elbows on my knees and hanging my head low.

Squatting down so that we are eye level, he brushes the hair out of my face. "Just breathe baby," he whispers. "You're doing so good."

"I-I can't do t-this..." I manage to gasp out.

"Yes, you can. You're the strongest and bravest woman I know, Rosalind Olivia," he murmurs softly. "You can do this." At his words, I can feel the anxiety lessening. It's not gone completely, and I guarantee I will throw up before I get to class, but it's enough to where I'm not gasping for breath anymore.

"Yeah, we have you, Rose. We aren't going to let anything happen to you," Amelia says. My head snaps up as I see her and Trevor standing behind Atticus, both with worried expressions.

Atticus brings my attention back to him. "Come on honey, we have to get to our first class. Trevor and Amelia will be with you during your first class, and I have the other two with you," he says as he cups my cheek.

"What about my class at noon?" I ask, picking at my fingers.

"I will just be late to mine," Atticus answers, after clearing his throat.

Running my hands over my face, I let out a huff. "Let's go before I change my mind," I say, sliding out of the seat. When my feet touch the ground, I sway a little, my head still swimming from the panic attack. Atticus is immediately there, steadying me.

"Are you sure you want to go to class today?" Trevor asks, looking at me over Atticus's shoulder.

"I have no choice. These classes are important for my degree," I say with a frown.

"Are you ready?" Atticus asks, squeezing my hand.

Before I can back out and ask him to take me home, I find myself nodding. "Let's go."

He studies me for a moment before reluctantly leaning down to give me a soft kiss. "I love you, Rosalind. I will see you next class, okay?"

"I love you, too. Have a good morning," I say before turning to Trevor and Amelia. We walk to class in silence, neither of them really knowing what to say. I have to stop at a trash can along the way. I knew I wouldn't make it. Amelia rubs my back while Trevor stands awkwardly to the side, glaring at people who gave me a second look. When I finish, Amelia hands me a tissue from her purse, and I thank her.

"I hate to be pushy," Trevor says, "but we need to get going."

Once we get to our class, I do a quick glance around the room. No sign of Derek yet, thank goodness. We walk to our seats, Trevor and Amelia sitting on either side of me.

Just as I'm hoping maybe his teammate was wrong, I hear the voice that haunts my dreams. "Trevor. Ladies," Derek greets as he goes to sit beside Trevor. Amelia's hand immediately finds mine under the desk. She squeezes gently and whispers something to me, but I can't hear it over the sound of the blood whooshing in my ears.

Trevor kicks the chair out from under Derek while glaring at him. "Find somewhere else to sit, asshole." Derek goes to protest, but the professor comes in at the perfect time and tells everyone to take a seat. Grumbling, he goes to sit on the other side of the room.

During the lecture, I catch Derek glaring at me. Not wanting to give him any more power than he already has, I sit up straighter and turn my focus back to the professor. Even though I'm not looking directly at him, I can always tell when he's looking at me.

Just as I'm starting to feel that familiar suffocating feeling, the professor dismisses us. I grab my supplies and rush out the door, with Trevor and Amelia right behind me. Opening the door to the building, I take in a deep breath of fresh air. "How the hell am I supposed to do this for an entire semester?" I say, turning to look at my friends. "I barely made it through that lecture, and I'm not sure I would have if it wasn't for you guys."

"Hey honey," Atticus says, coming up beside me and kissing my cheek. The distress must be visible on my face because he looks from me to Trevor. "What happened?" he asks.

Trevor fills him in on what happened while I lean against the building with Amelia at my side. She's trying to make small talk, but I just don't have it in me. It's taking everything I have just to get through today. "I'm sorry, Amelia, I just can't do this right now," I say as I make my way toward Atticus.

Chapter Twenty-One

Atticus

Seeing Rose walking over to me, I give Amelia a sympathetic smile. I know she just wants her best friend back. We all do. Putting my arm around Rose, I kiss the top of her head before telling Trevor bye. "Ready to go?" I ask as we walk away from our friends.

"Go home and go to bed? Yes. Go back to class and see Derek again? No." Her voice is low, and she is fidgeting with the hem of her shirt. "I don't want to do this anymore, Attie," she whispers.

Those words chill me to the bone. It's the same thing Kayla said in her suicide note. "What do you mean, Rose?" I ask, as I stop in my tracks and drop my arm from around her shoulders. She looks up at me and studies my face for a moment before the realization hits her.

"I mean school, Attie. I don't want to do school anymore," she clarifies. "If I'm just going to have to look over my shoulder every time I turn around, or if I'm going to need buffers to walk me to and from each class, I don't want to do it."

The frustration is clear on her face. She isn't used to being the one that needs help. She's the one that does the helping. It breaks my heart that she is in this position. "Can you do online classes until we get this figured out?"

"That would keep me from falling behind..." she reaches for my hand, and I lace our fingers together.

"Do you want me to go with you to talk to your advisor?" I ask, and she shakes her head.

"No, she wouldn't let you in with me. She's very big on student privacy," she says and rolls her eyes.

"Are you sure? I can at least walk you to her office?" I offer, and she shakes her head again.

"You will be late for class. I'm just going to the student center. I will be okay," she assures me.

Reluctantly, I sigh and squeeze her hand. "Alright, I will see you after class. Meet me at my car and I will take you home, okay?"

"Thank you, Attie," she whispers as she stands on her tiptoes to kiss my cheek.

"Call me if you need me," I tell her before she turns around and walks away. I watch her for as long as I can before she disappears behind the tree line next to the student center. Then I make my way to class.

Time drags by as the professor goes over the syllabus. Why can't they just let us read it on our own? Finally, she dismisses us, and I gather my things, rushing out the door to meet Rose. As I near my Jeep, I see Rose talking to two other girls. Her back is to me, but one look at the other two tells me this is not a pleasant conversation. Their faces are twisted in disgust. Getting closer, I realize they are part of a group of jersey chasers. We see them at every game, picking out their next target.

"Hey baby," I say as I approach, making sure Rose knows I'm behind her, so I don't scare her. "Ladies." I nod, not giving them a second glance.

"Hi Atticus," the brunette, I think her name is Morgan, says while batting her eyelashes.

Without glancing in her direction, I put my arm around Rose and smile down at her, "Ready to go?" When she nods, I turn back to the girls, "If you'll excuse us, my girlfriend and I are going home to enjoy all our free time since I am no longer on the basketball team." Their mouths drop open. I'm sure they're not used to getting rejected. It's no secret that I was kicked off the team. Half of the campus heard about it before noon the day it happened.

Rose looks up at me and smirks. "They took that well."

"Oh yeah. What did they want?" I ask as I open her door for her.

"Well, they were already here when I got to the car. Apparently, they were waiting on you and I was a disappointing surprise," Rose explains as she climbs in the car.

Once we are both inside, I start the car and head toward my house. At a red light, I glance over at Rose. She's looking out the window, and I smile softly before reaching over to grab her hand. She jumps somewhat, but turns and gives me a smile in return.

"You are so beautiful," I murmur just as the light turns green. When we get to my house, I open her door for her and we walk in. She sits her purse and books down on the counter and then walks over to me.

"Can we order pizza?" she asks, giving me the sweetest smile.

"Of course," I say, pulling out my phone. After I place our order, I grab her hand and pull her closer. "How did your meeting with your advisor go?"

"It went well. I told her that I needed to take some personal time off and asked if we could switch all possible classes to online. Luckily, since it was just the first day of the semester, it was still within the drop or transfer period," she says, wrapping her arms around my neck.

"Good," I say before leaning down and pressing my lips to hers. "Are you feeling better now that you got switched?"

"Much. I know I can't hide forever," she says with a sigh, "but right now, until I start seeing a therapist regularly and working through this, I think it's the best option."

"I'm so proud of you," I murmur, gently rubbing her cheek with my thumb.

"Thank you," she says softly. "I've been researching therapists, and I have an appointment with one tomorrow to see if she is a good fit."

"That's amazing, baby," I say with a beaming smile.

There's a knock at the door. "That must be the pizza," she says excitedly, going to grab two plates and water.

I realize that since she was so nervous this morning, she didn't eat. Then she threw up on her way to class. She must be starving. Going to the door, I grab the pizza and give the delivery guy his tip. After sitting the pizza down on the coffee table, I sit beside her on the couch.

Without saying a word, we dig in and enjoy the meal in comfortable silence. After finishing off three slices of pizza, Rose leans back into the couch, patting her stomach.

"Man, I am stuffed," she says as she looks up at me.

I laugh softly and finish my piece. Turning to look at her, I take in how relaxed she looks as opposed to this morning. She's not as tense as she was, and her smile is back. It may not be that same megawatt smile that I used to get, but it's a start.

Chapter Twenty-Two

Rosalind

"Good luck today," Atticus says as he kisses the top of my head. He's going to class, and I'm heading to meet with my potential therapist.

"Thank you," I say, turning so I can give him a quick kiss. "Have a good day. I will text you when I'm out of my appointment."

"Love you, honey," Atticus says as he turns to leave.

"I love you too!" I call after him. Looking back at my reflection, I sigh. The dark circles have started to fade, and I look more human than I have in the last two weeks. Instead of sweatpants and a hoodie, I have on leggings and a sweater. My hair is down and straight for the first time in forever. After giving myself another once over, I decide that's good enough and grab my keys off the dresser.

When I arrive at the therapists' office, I sit in the lobby and scroll through social media, waiting to be called back. I'm about to put my phone away when I get a text message notification.

Confused because everyone I talk to is in class, I open the message.

Going online won't stop me from keeping my promise. You shouldn't have told your boyfriend.

My stomach instantly goes sour, and I feel my breakfast about to come up. My heart is flying. *How the hell did he get my phone number?*

As I shakily slide my phone back in my purse, a lady steps out and calls my name. Standing, I follow her into the hallway and back to her office.

After sitting, she introduces herself, and then starts asking me questions about myself. I answer them haphazardly, but my mind is elsewhere. I can't shake the dreadful feeling that text has given me. All the happiness I was feeling about being less apprehensive has disappeared. I can't think straight, and I feel like an ass when the therapist, Misty, clears her throat.

"Ms. Johnson," she says, "You seem like you're in a completely different place." Her tone isn't harsh or condescending, but genuine.

I quickly shift my gaze to the floor and pick at my hands before shaking my head. I know that she is just trying to help, and that's literally her job, but it was hard enough telling Atticus and Amelia about what happened. How am I supposed to tell a complete stranger?

She raises an eyebrow before speaking again. "I'm here to listen to anything you want to share. Anything you say is completely confidential unless you are a danger to yourself or others."

Looking back up at her, I study her face. She's older, with wrinkles beginning to form, and her hair is slightly gray. There's something about her that just screams comfort, and for the first time in a long time, I find myself thinking about my mom. She was never this open and inviting. Even before my dad left.

"It's hard for me to talk about," I say before biting my lip. "But I guess I can start with why I decided to see a therapist," I begin. Once the words start flowing, I can't stop them. I tell her all about the attack, the panic attacks and nightmares, and Atticus getting kicked off the team for fighting Derek.

When I finish, I glance down at my hands. They're shaking and my heart is flying. I can't believe I just trauma dumped on my brand-new therapist. I know they say you can't really trauma dump in therapy, and she does this for a living, so I'm not the first nor the last person to do it to her, but it's still embarrassing.

"I appreciate you trusting me enough to tell me this," she says as she gives me a reassuring smile. "I can't imagine how difficult this must be for you."

"Other than my boyfriend and best friend, you are the only other person I've told," I say before looking back up at her.

The session continues as she helps me talk through what happened yesterday morning. We don't really touch on the attack yet. Our focus, for now, is what's happening in the present. She's just giving me some tools to help cope with the panic attacks and the nightmares. Before I know it, the hour has passed, and our time is up.

"Let's start with once a week visits, and then we can adjust based on your needs," she says while handing me a business card. "Here is my information in case you need it." I take the card from her and put it in my purse. Hopefully, I'll never need it, but it's better to be safe. As I stand to leave, she hands me a sticky note. "Here is the phone number to a psychiatrist that I work closely with. I think that you would benefit from at least meeting with her to hear what she has to say."

Thanking her, I grab the note and exit. Walking to my car, I pull my phone out and go to add the phone number for my therapist and the psychiatrist, but when I see a new message notification, I stop dead in my tracks. It's from Derek again. Taking a deep breath, I open the message and almost drop my phone. It's a picture of my car... in the parking lot at my therapist's office.

There's no message attached, only the photo. I frantically search around the parking lot, looking for any sign of Derek. He's nowhere to be found, so I rush to my car and get in, locking the doors. Even though we just went over some tips to help lessen panic attacks, I can't think of a single thing that was said. Hands shaking, I pick up my phone and dial Atticus's number.

Chapter Twenty-Three

Atticus

My professor glares at me when my phone starts vibrating on my desk. I give an apologetic smile before grabbing it. There's only one person that would be calling me right now. I jump to my feet and rush out of the room, leaving my stuff behind.

"What's up, baby?" I ask, concern lacing my words.

"H-he was here," she breathes out, fear evident in her voice.

"What? What do you mean? How do you know?" At this point, I'm ready to head out to my Jeep to go get her. "Where are you?"

"I'm at my therapist's office. I-I checked my phone when I got out and there was a picture of my car from his number." She explains. "I don't need you to come to me. I will be okay. I just needed to hear your voice before I had a total panic attack."

"Are you sure?" I question as I look in the window of the classroom door. Trevor catches my eye and I gesture for him to grab my stuff. He gives me a nod and I walk out of the building to the parking lot. She may not want me to meet her at her therapist's, but I can meet her at home.

"Yes, I'm sure. I already feel a little better. I'm sorry I called you during class," she mumbles.

"No, baby, don't apologize to me. I told you to call me when you needed me, no matter what." Starting the Jeep, my phone kicks over to Bluetooth. "I will meet you at home, okay?"

"Okay," she says, exhaustion evident in her voice. Just as we go to hang up, she speaks again. "Atticus."

"Yeah, babe?" I question.

"I love you," she says softly.

"I love you too. Be careful on your way home," I say before hanging up the phone.

I spend the drive to my house running through different scenarios. What if Derek had been waiting for her when she got out of her appointment? What if he follows her home? He knows where I live, and I'm sure he knows that she is staying with me.

Pulling into my driveway, I let out a sigh of relief as I see her car already here. It's empty, so she must be inside. Jogging up the steps, I open the door and step inside. "Rose?" I call out, walking through the house, trying to find her. As I reach the bedroom, I see her tiny frame curled up underneath a huge pile of blankets.

"Hey baby," I say as I climb in behind her.

"Hi," she murmurs as she slides over to me, burying her face in my chest.

My arms wrap around her on instinct, and I kiss the top of her head. "How did your appointment go today?" I ask as I run my fingers through her hair.

"It went well. I started talking and I couldn't stop. She also gave me the number to a psychiatrist that she thinks I should see," she said, her words muffled. My phone rings and Rose groans. "Tell them to go away."

Looking at my screen, I chuckle softly. "It's just Trevor. He's probably calling to see why I rushed out of class. I'll be right back," I say, climbing out of bed and walking to the hallway.

As I fill Trevor in on what Rose called me about, I hear him cursing on the other end of the phone. He tells me that Amelia mentioned Derek wasn't in class with her earlier. I sigh heavily. "Let's just keep that between us right now," I whisper to him, making sure to keep my voice down. The last thing Rose needs right now is more stress.

Hanging up with Trevor, I head back to the bedroom. Upon entering, the sight in front of me causes me to smile. Rose is sitting up against the headboard with a book in her hands and her computer in front of her. She glances up at me and gives a shy smile.

"I'm sorry. I was just trying to get some work done that I missed today," she explains.

"No need to apologize, honey," I tell her as I sit on the other side of her. "You do what you gotta do. Amelia and Trevor want to come over for game night later, if that's okay with you?"

"Of course, I think it would be good for me," she says before returning to her work.

Turning on the TV I lean back, resting my hand on her thigh. There's just something about her that makes me want to touch her all the time. Holding her hand, running my fingers through her hair, hand resting on her thigh, it doesn't matter as long as I can feel her.

As she continues to work, I think about what to do with the Derek situation. She doesn't want someone with her twenty-four seven, and I get that. But her safety is more important. I don't want to bring it up yet, maybe after Trevor and Amelia leave.

"You're going to get frown lines if you keep your face scrunched like that," Rose teases from beside me. Lost in my thoughts, I hadn't noticed that she finished working and put her laptop away.

"Sorry babe, just a lot on my mind," I say before leaning over to kiss her softly.

"Wanna talk about it?" She asks innocently.

"No, I'm okay. Do you want to go get the games out of the closet and I will see how far away Trev-" I'm cut off by the doorbell. "Well, it seems they're here," I say with a laugh before getting out of bed.

Rose goes to get the games, and I open the door for our friends. The smell of our favorite Chinese restaurant follows them as they step inside. "We brought food," Amelia says, holding up the bags.

"Oh great, I'm starving!" Rose exclaims from the hallway.

Trevor and Amelia make themselves at home after unloading the food onto the counter. Everyone grabs a plate and digs in, piling their plates full. As we sit down at the table, Amelia grabs the seat beside Rose.

Immediately, I notice that Rose is engaging a little more with Amelia than she has been in the last few weeks, so that makes me smile. I look over at Trevor and he is watching them too, the same smile on his face.

Chapter Twenty-Four
Rosalind

Making small talk with Amelia seems to be going better now that my secret is out. Before I was worried about slipping up and her finding out. I've missed my best friend. She's rambling on about something that happened in one of her classes today when I catch Atticus staring at us. I give him a small smile and he returns it with a wink.

Game night goes off without a hitch. Like always, the boys win, and Amelia and I get our asses handed to us. Once our friends leave, Atticus and I clean up the kitchen. I'm putting up the last dish when Atticus walks up behind me and wraps his arms around my waist. He leans down and kisses my neck, causing me to giggle.

"Atticus," I say, closing the cabinet before I turn in his arms. "What do you think you're doing?" Looking up at him, I see the mischievous gleam in his eye.

"Can't I kiss my girlfriend?" He innocently asks.

"You can." Leaning up on my tiptoes and sliding my hands around his neck, I pull his face closer.

His hands move to rest on the counter behind me, caging me in. My heart starts to race, and my breath hitches. He must sense the shift in my demeanor because he takes a step back, looking at me with yet another concerned expression. I don't mean to be like this, but being trapped like that causes my fight or flight instinct to kick in.

Sliding away from him, I turn and go to the bedroom, shutting the door behind me and locking it. I just need a moment to gather my thoughts and breathe. Atticus must have followed me because I hear a soft knock at the door, followed by his voice. "Rose... I'm sorry baby, I didn't realize what I was doing."

Listening to his words, I slump against the door, rubbing my face. "Just give me a few minutes, please."

"Five minutes and then I'm coming in." I listen to the sound of his footsteps retreating.

Sure enough, five minutes later, his footsteps return and another he knocks on the door again. "Open up, babe."

Opening the door, I keep my eyes on the floor. "I'm sorry that my body reacted that way," I whisper softly. "It's just... being pressed against the counter and your arms positioned like that caused my anxiety to heighten," I explain, looking up at him. The look on his face is quickly replaced with a mix of sadness and anger.

"It's not your fault," he assures me, reaching out to tuck a strand of hair behind my ear. "It's his fault, and mine... I wasn't thinking. I never want you to feel trapped like that again. I want you to lead us at your pace."

"I know, but I'm sure you wish you had a girlfriend that could be kissed without having an anxiety attack or sleep a full night without screaming like a lunatic," I mumble, looking up at him with unshed tears.

"Don't cry honey," He whispers as he reaches out and cups my cheek. "Listen to me," he says, wiping away a tear that has managed to escape my eyes. "If I could have any woman on this earth, I would still choose you. It doesn't matter who they are, what they have or haven't been through..." he trails off for a moment, leaning down to kiss my lips softly, "it will always be you. Always."

As he speaks, I can't stop the tears that slowly fall from my eyes. *How did I get so lucky to have this man in my life?* Taking his hands in mine, I squeeze them gently and lean up, kissing his cheek. "I don't think I would be able to make it through this without you," I whisper softly before I glance over at the time.

"I'm going to go take a shower, and then we can watch a movie in bed?" I suggest with a raised eyebrow.

"Well, there's actually something I need to talk to you about..." Atticus stops and rubs the back of his neck, "I didn't want to tell you before Trevor and Amelia got here, but when Trevor called earlier, he told me that it was Derek that was there today, and not one of his friends doing his dirty work for him."

I take a step back from him and close my eyes, taking in a deep breath. "You didn't think it'd be important to tell me?" I ask, before opening them and studying his face. "This is what was on your mind earlier when I asked if you wanted to talk about it and you said no."

He looks at me with regret in his eyes, shoving his hands in his pants pocket. "I didn't want to upset you before they got here," he says as he looks down at the floor. "I thought it was the better choice. I was going to talk to you about it now."

As much as I want to yell at him for keeping it from me, I know that he really was doing what he thought was best. I take a deep breath and then slowly let it out. "Okay," I say, leaning against the counter with my arms across my chest. "So, what do we do?" I ask.

"I'm not quite sure, since you don't want to report it." I immediately start to get defensive, but Atticus holds up his hand, "That is your decision I'm not shaming you for not reporting it," he clarifies, "but I was thinking, since I'm not busy with basketball all the time now, what if we try boxing? It will keep me in shape, and it will help you be able to defend yourself if you ever get caught in a position like that again."

Nodding as he tells me his suggestion, I run my hands over my face. "I can give it a try," I tell him, and can't help but smile at the relief and happiness that spreads across his face.

"Thank you, baby," he says as he walks over, kissing the top of my head. "Now, go shower. I'll pick the movie."

When I get in the bathroom, I turn the water on and undress. Looking at myself in the mirror as the water heats up, I'm surprised to see that I'm actually smiling. The bruises are long gone, and the cuts have healed for the most part. Getting in the shower, I sigh as the warm water runs over me. It has been a long day, and I can't wait to crawl into bed and cuddle up to Atticus.

Chapter Twenty-Five

Atticus

After we watch our movie, Rose falls asleep quickly. I have my arm around her, and she's tucked up against my chest. Listening to her steady breathing while I lie awake staring at the ceiling, my train of thought is like grand central station.

I find myself thinking of my parents. I wish more than anything that I could call my dad. He always knew exactly what to say, and I know he would have the perfect advice for me. Unfortunately, I lost both of my parents in a car accident not long after I started college. It's what caused Kayla's downward spiral before she tried to take her life, and why I was red-shirted for a season. I needed to be there for her. Life has a funny way of working out because if it hadn't been for me getting red-shirted, I wouldn't have met Rose.

Keeping her safe is my top priority, but then there's also the investigation at the school. My parents made sure my sister, and I were well taken care of before they passed, so I'm not worried about them kicking me out of school. I can find another online, or Rose and I can get the hell out of here. I can only hope that they let me stay and finish the rest of the semester out. If I get expelled, Rose will never forgive herself.

Rose shifts beside me in bed, throwing her leg over mine. I chuckle softly and kiss the top of her head. After our conversation earlier, we decided that it would be a good idea to start checking out gyms. I'm so glad that she took me up on my offer. It puts my worrying at ease just a little.

The next morning, I wake up alone. Just as I start to wonder where Rose is, the smell of bacon wafts through the open bedroom door. Throwing the covers back, I get out of bed and make my way to the kitchen. When I round the corner, I take in the sight before me, and the biggest smile crosses my face. Rosalind is standing at the stove singing to herself while she flips pancakes.

I walk over and lean against the counter off to the side, my arms crossed over my chest. Rose turns to greet me. "Good morning, handsome," she says with a huge smile.

"Morning, baby," I say as I lean over and kiss her cheek. "Anything I can do?"

"Can you grab us something to drink?" she asks as she sits the food on the table.

I nod and grab the orange juice out of the fridge before grabbing two glasses and taking it over to the table. The food smells so good my mouth is watering. I can't wait to dig in. Sitting down at my plate, I look up at her with a smile. "If this tastes as good as it smells... well, I'm just going to give up hopes of staying in shape," I say with a soft laugh.

"Oh, stop it," Rose says, blushing slightly. "Dig in. We have a busy day ahead of us," she adds before picking up her fork and cutting her pancake.

Once we are finished eating, I send her off to the bedroom to get ready while I do the dishes. After I finish, I go and throw on some clothes. Coming back out to the living room where Rose is now sitting, I grab my keys. "You ready?" I ask.

She nods and we head out to the car. The first gym we are going to is about fifteen minutes away. It's not too big, and they pride themselves in training beginners. I'm hoping they'll be a good fit.

When we arrive, it's not too crowded, which we both like. Rose looks over at me and gives me a nervous smile. I return the smile, but instead of nervousness, it's full of encouragement. "You got this, babe," I say before reaching for her hand. We walk into the gym and over to the front desk. The man, Gabe, his name tag says, takes our information, and we fill out some paperwork.

"Let me go see what trainers they want to pair you with," he says before he walks off into the main part of the gym. A few moments later, Gabe comes back and motions for us to follow him. Once inside the main gym, I look around. There are a few pairs sparring, a few at the heavyweight bags, and others doing agility drills.

"Rose, this is Ty. He will be your trainer," Gabe says, motioning to a man that comes to a stop beside him. Ty isn't the biggest guy here, but he definitely isn't the smallest. He appears to be about the same build as me, which is great, because so is Derek. We had briefly explained that we were looking for someone to help Rose learn some self-defense moves. Ty looks at Rose and nods, "Pleasure to meet you, ma'am," he says.

"Atticus, this is Brandon," Gabe says as he nods to the man on the other side of him. He is larger than Ty, but not by much. Instead of greeting me, Brandon gives a curt nod before motioning for me to follow him. I turn to give Rose one more wink before I walk away, leaving her with Ty and Gabe.

Chapter Twenty-Six
Rosalind

At first, I was a little nervous when Atticus left me standing with Ty. I was hoping that I would have a female trainer, but I know how important it is for me to have someone close to the same build as Derek.

We start off with some agility exercises and he shows me the correct form for a jab. It's not too complicated, yet. I seem to be getting the hang of it, and Ty seems pleased. The rest of the session goes by quickly. By the end of it, I'm exhausted, but I have never felt better. I can't wait to go home, take a nice long bath, and maybe talk Attie into rubbing my feet. Atticus. I realize I was so focused on my trainer that I hadn't seen Atticus since we parted ways.

My eyes search the gym and find him by the punching bags. After walking over to him, I lean up against the wall a few feet over, watching. When Brandon tells him he's good to go for the day, Atticus turns to look at me, grinning from ear to ear. I've only seen this smile on his face after basketball games.

"Hey, honey," he says, "ready to go?"

"Yeah, let's get out of here. I'm so sweaty and stinky," I say with a laugh.

Waving to Gabe on our way out, we make our way to the car. Once inside, we start the drive back to his house. Atticus clears his throat and glances my way, "So, I was thinking," he begins, "what if we stopped by your moms and grabbed your things to put at my house... permanently?" His hand goes to the back of his neck, rubbing it nervously.

"Atticus Michael, are you asking me to move in with you?" I ask with a teasing smile.

"I am," he says with a sheepish grin. "You're basically already living with me."

He makes a good point. I haven't been to my house since school started back. After a few moments of fake consideration, letting him squirm, I finally speak. "When do you want to get my stuff?"

I thought the smile from earlier was my favorite smile of his, but then when he hears my question, he smiles again and it's even bigger than the first smile. He passes up the exit to his house and takes the next one. "How about right now?" he asks.

Laughing, I shake my head. He's adorable. "Sounds great to me. My mom's at work." Sure enough, when we pull in, my mom's car is gone. Grabbing my keys out of the cupholder we head inside to grab what I want to take with me. Once we have finished packing things into bags and random boxes we have found, we load it into the back of his car. I leave mom a short note telling her that I'm going to stay with Atticus indefinitely, not that she would care, before going back out to the car and heading home.

Home. They say that when you're in love, you will understand what it means to view home as a person and not a place. Looking back over the last two years, I realize Atticus has been my home since the very first day.

I had longed for someone to care about me and my wellbeing. My mother sure didn't. Then when Atticus came along, he quickly became that person. He was always checking on me if I was sick, doing little things like bringing me tampons, or simply bringing me a 'Hey, I saw this and thought of you,' gift.

"Uh, Rose?" Atticus' voice snaps me out of my thoughts. "Where'd you go? I have been trying to have a full conversation with you, and you keep spacing out."

"Sorry, I was just thinking," I say, giving him a small smile.

"What were you thinking about so intently?" he asks with a raised eyebrow.

Reaching over for his hand, "That I love you more than you'll ever know," I say in a soft voice.

"I love you too, Rosalind," he says, giving my hand a squeeze before bringing it to his lips and kissing the back of it. "We're home," he adds.

I get out of the car and go up to the door, unlocking it and propping it open before going back out to the car to help Atticus bring my stuff in. We spend the night unpacking, and after my shower, I convince him to rub my feet while we watch Criminal Mind reruns on the couch.

The next three weeks come and go so quickly, I'm surprised as I pull into my fourth therapy session. Atticus has been going a little overboard with the protective boyfriend bit. Last week, he had a doorbell with a camera installed. I told him we didn't need one, but he insisted. Therapy has been going well. I've also started seeing the psychiatrist that Misty recommended, and surprisingly enough, I love boxing.

Getting out, I head inside and sign in. Just as I go to sit down, I'm called back. *Wow, they're on the ball today.* I follow her back to the office and begin our session. We have been mainly focusing on the present tense, only bringing up the attack whenever I feel like it's hindering my daily life. I am still having the anxiety and panic attacks, but with the tools Misty has been giving me, I'm beginning to work through them a little better. It's only been a month of therapy, and I know healing doesn't happen overnight, but the small progress gives me hope.

I've been back and forth on something for the last few days, and after talking with Misty, I was able to come to a solid decision. Walking out of the building, I feel like I could throw up, but confident. Not being able to keep it to myself, I check the time and call Atticus. He should be getting out of class right about now.

He answers on the first ring, "Hey baby," he says.

"I'm doing it," I blurt out. "Misty set up another appointment for me at the end of the week to help talk through anything I need to unpack."

"Good for you, baby," he says. I can hear the smile in his voice.

"I'm on my way to the school now," I say as I start driving.

"I'll be here waiting for you. Drive safely, I love you," he says before disconnecting the call.

After my therapy session last week, and much back and forth, I had told Atticus that I wanted to make the report. With boxing building my confidence, and my therapy sessions helping my panic attacks, I decided I was tired of running. Derek got Atticus kicked off the team, and I switched to online only classes. It had been two months of torture, and it was time for me to take my life back.

The closer I get to school, the more my nerves seem to take hold. Trying some of the breathing exercises we talked about in therapy, I park beside Atticus. As soon as I put it in park, he throws my door open and gives me a smile. I take a deep breath in and let it back out, closing my eyes for a moment. Then, with a nod, I get out of the car.

"Ready to do this?" he asks as he holds his hand out for me to take once I'm beside him.

Taking his hand, I squeeze it gently, afraid if I speak, I will talk myself out of it.

Chapter Twenty-Seven

Atticus

"Ms. Johnson, you know this is a serious accusation you are making, correct?" Dean Smith says as he stares at her over the top of his glasses. I'm standing behind her against the wall, and she is sitting in front of his desk. I can't see her face, but I can tell that she wants to retreat by the way her body language changes, but just as quickly, she recovers. She sits up taller, pushing her shoulders back, and damn, I am so proud. "You are claiming that Derek Murphy physically and sexually assaulted you two months ago after the scrimmage at the beginning of the season?"

"Yes, I understand, and yes, that is correct," Rose says as she grips the arm of the chair.

"Why did you not make a report sooner? Surely, if what you say is true, you would have done so already." He leans forward in his chair, propping his hands on his desk.

Before Rose can respond, I step forward from behind, "With all due respect, sir, what we are not going to do today is victim blame. Rosalind is coming to you to report crimes that a student has committed on this campus, and you are not going to make her feel less than because she waited to report it. Seeing as how the statute of limitations have not expired, Rosalind still has the right to report it." I say as I place my hand on her shoulder to comfort her.

She reaches up and pats my hand in a silent thank you, and I step back against the wall. The dean has turned his attention to me. "Ah, Mr. Reed," he says, "I recall you also have issues with Mr. Murphy."

"This is not about me or my issues with him. This is about what happened to Rose," I remind him.

"Yes, well, we will look into these claims and get back to you," he says before he stands. "Now, if you'll excuse me, I have a board meeting to get to."

Rose goes to stand up but freezes when she hears him mention the board meeting. She looks back at me and I know what's going through her mind. Derek's parents usually attend the board meetings. She recovers and stands, reaching for my hand. I take it as we follow Dean Smith out of the room.

"I will talk with the other party involved and get their side," he says as he turns to face us.

"Thank you for meeting with us," Rose mumbles, and I squeeze her hand gently before pulling her out of the office and out to the parking lot. I don't stop until we are beside the car, and I turn her to look at me. Tears are heavy in her eyes as she sniffles, "I don't know why I did that," she murmurs. "It's not going to help anything. They're probably going to kick me out of school now for a false claim."

"Rosalind," I say, pulling her to my chest. "That was the bravest thing you could have done. I am so proud of you. I know that you're worried about the outcome, but let's focus on this win right now."

She leans into me and lets out a heavy sigh. "Let's go home. I want to take a nice bath."

"Okay honey. Let's go. I will drive and when Trevor and Amelia come over for game night later, they can stop and grab your car," I tell her, and she nods.

I can tell that Rose is distracted during the quiet drive home. She hasn't even turned on her music, which is not like her at all. When we get home, I open her door for her, and she slips her hand in mine as we walk inside. Shutting the door behind us, I turn to face her.

"Hey, I will go start your bath, and then you can come get in when you're ready," I say, looking at her, and she nods. Going into the bathroom, I fill the tub up and add her favorite bubble bath to it. Smirking as the familiar vanilla scent fills the air.

Rose shuffles into the bathroom with her robe on and stands beside the tub. Glancing over at her as I stand from the tub, I stop in my tracks. She's been crying, and it absolutely breaks my heart. I wish there was a way to take all her pain away. Instead, I do the only thing I can and pull her into my arms. Exhaling as I pull her against me, I lean down and kiss the top of her head.

"Take your bath and then we can cuddle," I murmur into her hair before letting her out of my embrace and leaving the bathroom to give her privacy.

After changing into sweats, I walk into the kitchen and get her cookies and a glass of chocolate milk, her favorite comfort foods. Taking them into the bedroom, I sit them on the nightstand on her side of the bed. Glancing at the time, I pull my phone out and call Trevor. I tell him we need to reschedule game night and ask if they can still drop Rose's car off for us. It's been a long day and I know Rose won't be up for any visitors. He agrees and says he will just put the keys in my Jeep.

We talk for twenty minutes while he tells me about how the team is doing, and how practice went today. Derek was there and never mentioned anything about the accusations Rose made, so either they haven't told him yet or they're just dismissing them. When we finally hang up, I lay back on the bed. Rose's baths usually last anywhere from fifteen to twenty minutes because as soon as the water starts getting cold, she hates it. Looking at the clock, I notice it's been over thirty minutes.

I go to the bathroom door and knock twice. "Hey baby, are you about done?" I call through the door. No answer. Maybe she didn't hear me?

Knocking again, I wait for her to reply. Still no answer. *Fuck, Rose. Say something.*

"I'm coming in, Rose," I say before twisting the handle and stepping inside.

Chapter Twenty-Eight

Rosalind

Ever since we got out of our meeting with Dean Smith, I haven't been able to think straight. *Did I just mess everything up? Are they going to just smack Derek on the wrist and send him on his way? Will they even mention it to him, or am I going to be swept under the rug?* This all runs through my head as I sit in the bathtub.

I'm aware of the fact that the bubbles are disappearing, and the water is getting colder. I just can't bring myself to get out. I try to focus on the tips my therapist gave me to deal with situations like this, but I can't. I don't want to do anything but the one thing I can control. I reach over the side of the tub and grab my robe, fishing the item I'm looking for out of my pocket.

Just as I'm about to fall into the familiar darkness, I hear Atticus's voice in my head telling me he loves me. I stop and look down at the blade. He will be so disappointed. No, scratch that. *I* will be so disappointed. I am stronger than this.

Getting out of the tub, I dry off and put my robe back on. Then I lay the blade down on the counter and back away. Once my back hits the wall, I slide down and put my head in my hands. I hear Atticus outside the door, and I want to say something to let him know I'm okay. It's just, nothing is coming out. I have no energy left for anything. I'm tired. The kind of tiredness that you feel deep in your bones.

When Atticus opens the door, I pull my head from my hands. He comes to stand in front of me, before crouching down to be level with me.

"Talk to me baby, what's going on?" The worry that blankets his face is heartbreaking.

"I just... I am so tired, Atticus," I say quietly.

"We can go to bed?" he suggests.

"No, this is a tired that sleep isn't going to help..." I say before dropping my head back into my hands. "I know that you know about my rocky relationship with my mom, but you don't know all of it."

"Tell me about it, baby." He sits down on the floor beside me, pulling me into his arms.

"When my dad caught her cheating, and he left, she blamed me. Even though I wasn't home at the time, I was in school. Like a normal fifteen-year-old. She would get drunk and berate me every chance she got." Atticus listens intently as I talk. "It started off with simple things, like 'this is your fault' but escalated to 'you are worthless'. At fifteen, that's a lot to deal with. Plus, I was dealing with the fact that my dad just left me to fend for myself with her." I sigh before looking away from Atticus.

"After so long, you start to believe that, and the thoughts are all-consuming. So, to keep the demons away, I turned to the one thing I could control. Looking back now, I realize that it just hurt me more than helped. If I could go back and tell my younger self that it isn't worth it. I totally would," I say before wiping a tear from my eye.

"I dealt with that for a year and a half, then I met Amelia, which, in turn, led me to you. It's like you chased all the darkness away. I found myself not wanting to use that anymore." I gesture to the blade on the counter. "Then my feelings for you developed from friendship to more than friendship, and I was biding my time, waiting for you to make a move. Then when the thing with Derek happened, it was like no matter what, I couldn't find my way back to you." I look back over at him, and he reaches over, grabbing my hand.

"Slowly, you began to pull me out of my shell again, and I thought things were getting better. I felt like I was floating. Until something grabbed hold and drug me under today after I reported the assault and was essentially dismissed. I'm drowning and I don't know if I can resurface," I whisper before wiping my eyes before I lean my head against the wall.

"I'm so sorry that you have been dealt such a shitty hand," Atticus says as he gently turns me to look at him. "But I promise you that no matter what, I will not give up on you, Rosalind Olivia. I don't care how many times I have to dive into the darkness to pull you back out. I will do it. I don't know the exact moment that I fell in love with you, but I will tell you this. You're it for me."

I can't stop the new influx of tears that fall down my cheeks as I listen to him. He doesn't understand how much his words mean to me. I didn't know when Trevor introduced us that this brown-haired, blue-eyed boy would become the one to stand by my side and help chase away the darkness.

"Come on, let's go to the bedroom. I brought you some cookies and chocolate milk." I know he's trying his best to help lighten the mood, and I appreciate it.

I rub my hands over my face a few times, resetting my 'mask', before I look up at him with a hint of a smile. "Did you say cookies?" I ask.

He eyes me warily but helps me up from the floor. "Yeah, and chocolate milk."

"Thank you, Attie," I say as I stand. Looking over at the counter, I spot my blade. "Can you do something for me?" I ask, looking back at him.

"Anything," he says, giving my hand a squeeze.

"I'm going to leave the bathroom, and I need you to dispose of this." I gesture to the blade on the counter.

"How about..." he says, walking over and grabbing it before joining me again. "I stay with you while you do it. I think it will be healing in a way, if you do it yourself."

Nodding, I take it from his hand and walk into the kitchen. Sitting it on the counter, I open the junk drawer and pull out a tape dispenser. Carefully, I take a couple pieces of tape and wrap around the blade so that it isn't sharp anymore. Atticus keeps his hand on the small of my back throughout the entire process, reminding me that he is there. Once it's wrapped well, I go over to the garbage and toss it in.

"I'm so proud of you," Atticus says as he grabs the garbage bag and ties it up. "Go on and get your cookies, and I will be there as soon as I take this to the trash."

Nodding, I head to the bedroom and throw on a pair of underwear and one of his t-shirts. Sitting down in the bed, I lean against the headboard and pull the plate of cookies into my lap. I've eaten two by the time Atticus comes back and slides in beside me. He takes the plate from me and puts it on the nightstand before he pulls me into his lap.

I turn so that I'm straddling him and lay my forehead on his shoulder. "Thank you." I whisper softly.

"Are you feeling better?" His hands slide soothingly down my back and come to rest on my hips.

"I'm feeling a little better. I think I just need some sleep," I lie, not looking up at him.

"Well, let's get you to bed honey," he says as he moves me off his lap and back into the bed. "We are supposed to go train tomorrow, but if you don't feel like it, you don't have to go."

"We will see in the morning," I say as I turn on my side and scoot until my back is flush against his chest.

His arms go around me, and he kisses my head, holding me against him. "Goodnight, Rosalind. I hope you know how much I love you," he whispers in my ear.

"I love you too, Atticus. Goodnight," I say as a yawn escapes my lips.

Shortly after, I find myself falling into a deep sleep. A few hours later, I wake a little sweaty, and my mouth is dry. I must have had a mild nightmare. Slipping out from under Atticus's arm, I go to the kitchen and grab a bottle of water. As I turn to head back to the bedroom, movement outside the window catches my eye. I stop for a moment, trying to figure out what I saw, but since I don't see it again, I just chalk it up to being tired.

Climbing back in bed, Atticus groans and reaches for me, before pulling me back to my spot in his arms. I laugh softly and allow myself to drift back off to sleep. I'm hoping I feel better in the morning. I'm tired of being tired. I want to get better. I want to be the person Atticus deserves, but more importantly I want to be the person I deserve.

When I wake the next morning, Atticus is nowhere to be found. I sit up in bed and stretch. Last night was rough, but Atticus was right. I do feel a little better after resting. Yesterday took a lot out of me emotionally, which I believe is what caused my mini spiral. Making my way through the house, I glance at the wall clock in the kitchen. It's eleven thirty, so I can only assume that he is at the gym. Shrugging, I grab a mug out of the cabinet and make myself some coffee.

I hear the front door open and glance at the clock. "Home already?" I call out, but there's no answer. "Atticus?" I say, turning around to make my way to the living room. As I lift my eyes from my coffee, my breath hitches and I drop the mug in my hands.

"Hello, little Rose," Derek says with a sinister grin. "Did you think you could hide from me?" he asks as he closes the distance between us. The crunch of the mug as his shoes step on the pieces sends a chill up my spine.

"Derek, wh-what are you doing here?" I manage to rush out.

"I told you not to tell anyone," he seethes before grabbing hold of my arm.

Chapter Twenty-Nine

Atticus

After looking at his watch, Brandon tells me that's all the time we have for today's session. My entire body hurts. I have spent the last hour and a half really pushing it to its limits. Groaning, I make my way to my bag and sling it over my shoulder. I'll shower at home. I have been so frustrated with everything going on, and boxing has been a great outlet.

Pulling my phone out of my bag, I scroll through my notifications, none from Rose. *That's odd.* She should be up by now. It's twelve thirty. I do have a notification from the doorbell camera, though. The time stamp says motion was detected at eleven thirty-five. Maybe she ordered food?

I pull up the footage as I'm walking out to the lobby and when I see the cause of the notification, I stop abruptly. "What the fuck?" I practically shout.

"Hey man, is everything alright?" Gabe asks, coming out of an office.

"No, no, it is not. I have to go," I say as I rush out of the building and to my jeep. I throw it in reverse and speed out of the parking lot. He has been alone with her for almost an hour. I quickly call 911 and explain the situation briefly as I speed through town. The woman on the other end of the line tells me to stay outside and wait on the police, but I kindly tell her to fuck off before hanging up and dialing Trevor.

It rings twice before he picks up. "Hey man, wh-"

"Meet me at the house. Now." I interrupt him. I live fifteen minutes from the gym, but this drive feels like it's taking forever.

"What's going on?" he says, concern heavy in his voice.

"It's Rose. He got her, man. He fucking got her." My hands are gripping the wheel tightly.

"I'm on my way to Amelia now, we will be there soon," he says before adding, "and Atticus, I know what you're thinking, but you couldn't have prevented this."

How does he know me so well? As I hang up with him, I come to a screeching halt in the driveway before jumping out and running into the house.

"Rose!" I yell as I burst through the door. The house is a wreck. There's a broken mug in the kitchen. Decorations that were on the counters are strewn across the floor, but no sign of her. I begin to make my way further into the house and dread fills my stomach. As I step into the hall that leads to the bedroom, I stop dead in my tracks. There's a trail of blood.

My heart is pounding in my chest as I push the bedroom door open. There's nothing in here except more blood and broken glass. There's only one place left to look.

When I open the cracked bathroom door, the sight inside makes me drop to my knees. *No... please no...* Rose is lying in a crumpled heap on the floor. She whimpers and I scramble over to her, still on my hands and knees. There's glass everywhere from the shattered mirror, but I ignore the pain in my knees as it cuts them. The agony growing in my chest is more painful than anything I have ever experienced.

"Rose," I whisper out, tears pooling in my eyes. I tried to brush some of the hair out of her face, but the majority is caked in blood and stuck to her face. My mind is running a hundred miles per hour, but I feel like my entire world has come to a halt. My stomach churns as I take in her appearance. I notice her nose, which is undoubtedly broken, and a cut above her swollen left eye. On her neck, a bruise in the shape of a hand is forming again.

Trevor shouts from the front of the house, alerting me they've arrived, and I look from Rose to the door. Amelia cannot see her like this.

"Trev don't let Amelia back here," I yell out.

"Atticus, if you think for one second, I'm not coming to check on my best friend, you've lost your damn mind," Amelia yells back as I hear her struggling to get by Trevor.

"Amelia... I mean it. Stay. Put," I growl out. Trevor finally gets Amelia to stand out on the porch before he comes to find me.

"Holy... shit," he mumbles as he comes into the bathroom, "Is she..." he trails off and I know the question he doesn't want to ask.

Shaking my head, I look up at him, tears running down my face. "She's alive. She was whimpering when I got in here."

I want to just pull her into my arms, but with all the bruising and cuts, I don't want to hurt her even more. Although, at this point, I don't think that she would even notice. I just sit beside her, carefully running my hand over her hair.

"At... Att..." she moans.

"I'm here baby. I'm right here. Stay with me," I plead.

Judging by the commotion in the living room, the police have finally arrived. They find us quickly with Amelia's instructions and immediately I hear one of them calling for a medic.

I can't move. I feel like I have been rooted to the floor. All I can think about is what will happen to my heart if hers stops.

"Son, you have to let them through to work on her," one of the officers, Westbrook, tells me, snapping me out of my haze.

"I can't leave her," I whisper.

"If you can't move over so we can work on her, you will be hurting more than helping her. Let us do our job," the medic says as she comes up behind me.

"I'll just be right over here, baby," I tell her as I reluctantly stand and move to the side so the medics can get to her. The officer from before comes over to talk to me, but I can't really give him full answers. I'm too busy watching them work on Rose.

"Look," the officer says as he steps in front of me, blocking my view. "I understand that you care deeply for this woman, but the best thing that you can do for her right now is give us all the information you can about the attack."

I nod and focus on the man in front of me. When I tell him who her attacker was, his eyebrows shoot up. "Yes, I'm aware, serious accusations, et cetera, et cetera," I grind out, "we heard the exact same thing from the dean yesterday when she reported the previous assault."

"No, it's just the Murphy's are a well-known family. I don't know anything about the report, though. We didn't receive a notification," he says as he writes down some notes. "You said you have video footage of him entering the home? Do you have that video footage right now?"

Nodding, I feel around in my sweatpants for my phone. Pulling it out, I open the app and hand the phone over to him. The angle the camera is facing makes it easy to see that it is, in fact, Derek picking the lock to the house and slipping inside.

Speeding it up to the end, we see him coming out forty-five minutes later. He's rubbing his face, and as he turns to look down the street before running off, you can see that he has a split lip and a busted nose. I look past the officer again, and it's like I can feel my heart literally breaking.

After Rose is on the stretcher and they're taking her out of the house, I look at the medic, who is already answering the question on my face. "You can't ride with us, but you can meet us there."

Before they put her in the back of the ambulance, I lean down beside her ear, "You promised me you'd never leave me again, Rose," I whisper, "Please don't." The medic clears her throat. "I'm right behind you, baby. I love you so much," I whisper, wiping the tears from my eyes. After kissing her temple, I back away and let them put her inside.

"Come on, I'll drive," Trevor says from beside me, placing his hand on my shoulder. Honestly, I forgot he was even here, but man, am I thankful. I nod before following him to his car.

"Atticus," Westbrook shouts as he jogs over to me, "I know you're trying to get a move on, but I wanted to tell you I've contacted the manufacturer of the doorbell for them to send the video footage, so we have a copy."

"Thank you, man," I say as I open my door. "Now, if you'll excuse me, I have to get going."

He nods and steps back to where I can climb in Trevor's car. Amelia is sitting in the back seat. I glance at her as I get in the car, and she's white as a ghost. I can only imagine what seeing Rose like that has done to her. After buckling up, I reach back and take her hand. She looks up at me and the unshed tears in her eyes fall.

"She will be okay, you guys," Trevor says from the driver's seat. "It's Rose. She's tougher than the three of us combined." He adds. I'm not sure who he's trying to convince, us or himself. I let go of Amelia's hand and run my fingers through my hair. Catching a glimpse of her blood on my hands just makes my stomach churn. *Please, Rose, don't leave me.* I don't think my heart can take another loss.

The drive to the hospital feels like it takes eternity. As soon as the car is at a stop, I jump out and run through the emergency room doors. My hands are shaking as I lean against the desk.

"Can I help you?" the woman behind the desk asks.

"Rosalind Johnson," I breathe out, "I need to see her."

"Are you family?" she asks with a challenging raise of her eyebrow.

Just as I'm about to protest, Officer Westbrook comes around the corner, "Atticus," he nods and motions for me to follow him.

"They have taken her back to surgery," he says after taking me to the side. "After reviewing the raw footage from the security company, we have issued an APB for Derek Murphy," he adds, and I sag against the wall.

"Thank you," I murmur. Hearing my name, I look up and see Trevor and Amelia rushing my way. Westbrook nods and steps away, giving us privacy while he answers a phone call.

"Atticus," Amelia says breathlessly, "where is she?"

"She's in surgery," I tell them, as I close my eyes and lean my head back against the wall, letting out an exhale. Sliding down so I'm sitting on the floor, I begin to tell them everything. I tell them about what happened yesterday with the dean, and then her reaction when we got home. I proceed to tell them that I left her at home this morning because she was finally sleeping, and I didn't want to disturb her.

"I looked at my notifications after my boxing session and had no messages from her," I say, "then I saw the doorbell camera's notification and that's when I saw him. He broke in, and well, you saw for yourselves." I fist my hands in my hair, letting out a frustrated sigh. "They haven't told me anything else, except she is in surgery."

By this point, Amelia has joined me on the floor, and Trevor is crouched on the other side. Amelia takes my hand in hers and we sit in silence for a few moments. Neither of them really knows what to say, but them being there means more than any words they could say to me.

Chapter Thirty
Rosalind

What's that smell? I don't remember buying a candle that smells like... antiseptic? Shit, my head hurts. What is that beeping noise? Man, that's annoying. Am I in the hospital? Do I hear voices? Is that Atticus? Amelia? Who's that guy? Maybe I should wake up now. But I'm so tired. Then it comes back to me. *Derek broke into our house and came after me again.* As I recall the events, the monitor beside me starts beeping rapidly.

I'm vaguely aware of the commotion around me, and then everything is fading away again. The last thing I hear before the darkness fully takes me over is Atticus saying, "Just rest baby, you're okay. You're safe now. I'll be here when you wake up. I love you so much," then everything goes black.

༶

Sometime later, I find myself waking back up. Squinting against the bright fluorescent lights, I lift my hand to shield my eyes, and eye it with confusion when I see a cast.

"Rose?" a tired voice comes from beside me before the person leans into my line of vision. Atticus. My eyes lock on his, and the look of relief that crosses his face makes my heart clench. "Thank goodness," he whispers as he leans down and gently kisses my forehead. "I was so worried about you," he murmurs.

"Attie..." I whisper, my voice hoarse.

"I'm right here, baby. I'm not going anywhere," he promises.

Looking down at the cast on my hand, I glance back over at him. "What happened? I mean, I know that Derek broke into the house, but after that, I pretty much don't remember."

"That's because you have a concussion, well, that and your mind has probably repressed it to help your body heal physically first," a man standing in the doorway says, before coming into the room. "I'm Dr. Adams. I have been taking care of you for the last twenty-four hours."

"Twenty-four hours?" I question.

"The first couple of times you woke, you were in a state of panic. So, we gave you something to help you sleep. Atticus here," he says while gesturing to him, "has not left your side since we allowed him to see you after surgery."

I glance over at Atticus, who is already looking at me. The tiredness in his eyes and the way he's slouched on the side of my bed tells me the doctor is telling the truth. This man hasn't moved from my side.

"I'm not going to bother you long, I just wanted to come in and check on you before shift change, and I wanted you to hear from me the extent of your injuries," he says before he glances at Atticus, who gives him a nod.

"Okay," I say warily.

"So, aside from the concussion and the broken hand, I assume you have noticed by now," he says, "You have a broken nose, a few broken ribs, and one of the blows also caused your spleen to rupture. We had to go in and remove the spleen because it was irreparable. You also had a few lacerations that needed stitching."

After a few questions, and him going over our next steps, he exits the room. I look over at Atticus and tears fill my eyes. He stands abruptly and knocks his chair over, startling me.

"Shit, I'm sorry baby," he says as he sits his chair back up before coming to sit on the side of my bed. "Is there anything I can do for you?" he asks.

"Can you lay with me?" I ask softly, reaching up to wipe my eyes. "Fuck that hurt." I wince as my hand brushes over the tender black eye.

He eyes me carefully while chewing on his lip. "I don't want to hurt you," he whispers.

"You won't hurt me, please…" I whisper. I just need his arms around me.

He finally agrees and slips his shoes off before helping me slide over a little so he can lay beside me. I bite my lip to try to keep from groaning, but it still slips out. Atticus freezes and looks down at me. "I'm hurting you."

"No, I'm okay now," I assure him, as I reach for his hand. "Thank you…" I whisper as I drift off to sleep again.

Damn, this cast is annoying. My eyes open as I fight with the cords and my cast while trying to get comfortable again. *Why did it have to be my dominant hand that needed the cast?* Beside me comes soft snores, and I glance over, seeing Atticus sound asleep.

Looking up at the sound of the door open, I find myself smiling. Amelia and Trevor walk in, and Amelia is carrying a big bouquet of flowers. Atticus stirs beside me as he reaches for my hand. I slip my hand into his and rub the back of his hand with my thumb.

"I'm glad he's finally getting some sleep," Trevor says in a soft voice.

"Yeah, he has been an absolute wreck," Amelia adds. "I'm so glad you're okay."

I smile at our friends and nod, "Me too," I say, looking over at Atticus, who's starting to stir again. I pat his leg gently, letting him know that I'm still here and it quiets him again.

"Have the police been here yet?" Trevor inquires. "They've talked to Atticus a few times, keeping him updated on the case."

"No, I've only seen the doctor once, and the rest of the time I've been in and out of sleep," I say. "Do you think he will have any kind of consequences?"

"Well, they have footage of him breaking into your house, and then coming out shortly before Atticus came home." Trevor looks over at Amelia before looking back at me. "They've had an APB out for him since they got the footage. The officer yesterday was confused when Atticus mentioned the report you filed with the university because the school never reported it to them. Which in turn will bite the school in the ass since Dean Smith is a mandated reporter, and he failed to do so."

"So, they still haven't caught him yet?" I ask, and when he shakes his head I sigh, "Maybe mommy and daddy have him put up somewhere that they think no one will look."

Atticus clears his throat beside me, and I turn to look at him. "Good morning sleepy head."

"Morning babe," he replies, his voice husky. "How's your pain?" he asks as he slides out of the bed, and I frown.

"It's fine. Where are you going?" I ask with a pout.

He chuckles softly before kissing the top of my head. "Just to the bathroom, honey. I'll be back in two seconds."

While he's gone, I find the remote that controls the angle of my bed and sit myself up a little straighter. Letting out a soft groan, Amelia gives me a concerned look and I give her a reassuring smile. "It's okay. I'm fine." Moving seems to hurt every part of my body, but when I hear the door to the bathroom opening, I school my features and give Atticus a smile.

"Are you hungry?" I ask him, hopeful the pain doesn't show in my voice.

"I could definitely go for some food," he says, his eyes lingering on me for a moment before he looks at Trevor. "You wanna go check out the cafeteria?" To which Trevor nods and stands.

After telling him to surprise me with whatever, he grabs his phone and wallet, then hands me my phone before kissing me softly. "Call me if you need me honey,"

When he's gone, I look at Amelia and I can't stop the tears that finally fall. She is immediately by my side and grabs hold of my hand. "It's okay, Rose," she whispers as she runs a hand over my hair gently. "You know you don't have to be strong for him all the time, right?" she asks.

"The last few months he has had to be the strong one for the majority of the time," I tell her between sniffles. "I just don't want him to feel like he constantly has to deal with the broken, weak Rose."

"Well, sister, I think that your plan is backfiring." Amelia motions to my battered body, "Because if you think that he is going to do anything but take care of you right now, you're badly mistaken."

Neither of us say anything, and she silently holds my hand. My phone dings with a new message and I let go of Amelia's hand to open it. "The guys will be back in a second. They just got on the elevator," I tell her. She walks to the bathroom and wets a washcloth before bringing it to me. "Here," she says with a small smile.

"Thank you," I whisper as I gently wipe my face, damn it hurts.

Just as I give her the washcloth to take back to the bathroom, the guys walk in. "We are going to head out. We just wanted to drop these flowers off along with your car, and Amelia wanted to see if you were awake," Trevor says and Amelia smiles apologetically at me.

"Thank you for coming guys and thank you for being there for Atticus." My voice breaks a little as I look at my friends with complete gratitude. "I honestly don't know what I would do without you three."

Amelia walks over to me and grabs my non injured hand, before giving it a soft squeeze. "I love you, Rose," she says, wiping her eyes. She and Trevor say their goodbyes and walk out the door.

"Do you need help sitting up to eat?" Atticus asks as he sits food on the tray and slides it so it's over my lap.

"Yes, please." I ask and grab a fist full of the sheets. He comes over and uses the buttons on the side of the bed to raise the bed more. The movement causes me to gasp from the ache it sends through me, and the gasp causes me to cough. I reach out to grab ahold of Atticus' arm as I cry out in pain. "Fuck, that hurts so bad," I whimper.

Atticus looks over at the whiteboard and then walks over to my bed, hitting the nurse's call button. When they answer, he asks if they can bring something to help with the pain. Not long after they disconnect, there's a knock at the door and a nurse walks in.

"Here you go dear," she says, scanning my bracelet and then the medication before she hands it to me.

"Thank you," I say, taking it and the bottle of water Atticus hands me.

After I take the medication, I attempt to eat the food that Atticus has brought, but I find myself growing tired again. Whatever they have me on has been knocking me on my ass. Looking over at Atticus, I give him an apologetic smile. "I can't eat anymore right now," I say softly.

He nods and pulls the tray away from the bed and then sits on the edge of the bed. "Go ahead and sleep baby, I'll be here when you wake," he says, reaching out to brush my hair out of my eyes. "I love you."

I give him a grateful smile before I lean the bed back a little, wincing in pain again, but it isn't as bad this time. "I love you, too," I whisper before I close my eyes and drift off to sleep.

"You can run, but you can't hide," Derek seethes as he holds his now broken nose. Thanks to Ty and his training, I was able to get a few jabs in, effectively breaking his nose, but also probably my hand. Stumbling into the bathroom, I turn to lock it but he's already got his foot in the door, preventing me from closing it.

"Now is that any way to treat your houseguest?" Derek says as he advances me again. Grabbing me by the back of my head, he smashes my head into the mirror.

"Derek, please, I will recant my statement," I plead.

"Too late, they've already kicked me off the team," he says as he yanks my head back.

I jolt awake, gasping. I can't breathe deep enough to calm down, and I feel like I'm suffocating. I look to where Atticus was sitting when I fell asleep, and his chair is empty. Where did he go? My heart rate is skyrocketing, and I still can't breathe well. Suddenly, the door opens and in comes a nurse, followed by a frantic Atticus.

Atticus immediately comes to my side. "They're going to help, baby," he whispers as he reaches for my hand.

The nurse puts something in my IV and I look over at Atticus, panic in my eyes. "I don't want to sleep… he's there."

The look on Atticus' face is full of sorrow. "I know baby, I know. Your body needs the rest, though."

As he talks, I feel my eyelids growing heavy. "Atticus," I whimper as I drift back off to sleep.

Chapter Thirty-One
Atticus

After Rose drifts off to sleep, I rub her hand gently. I could tell she was in the middle of a nightmare when she started grabbing at her neck, which happens often. It's already hard enough for her to breathe without being in pain, so deep breathing to calm the panic attack would have been excruciating. I tried to catch it before she was hyperventilating and was almost too late.

Watching her sleep for a few minutes, I finish eating my burger and then clean up from dinner. I look over at Rose after sitting down in the reclining chair they brought me last night. The bruising on her body is beginning to turn black and blue, and her black eye is starting to swell a little more. The Dr. said that it will probably peak tomorrow, and not to worry if it looks worse.

I lean my head back and close my eyes. I wish like hell I would have taken her with me to the gym. She has been through so much in the last few months. I'm amazed at how incredibly strong she is. I haven't told her yet, but her dad is on his way here. As soon as I called him, he rearranged his schedule and started the drive here. They haven't seen each other in a while, and I know that Rose will be excited. Despite living thirteen hours away, her dad dropped everything and came when his daughter needed him, whereas her mother, who lives only thirteen minutes away, couldn't be bothered.

Unintentionally, I fall asleep to the steady beeping from her monitor. When I wake again, Rose isn't in her bed. Alarmed, I shoot out of the chair. She isn't supposed to be up moving by herself. Just as I'm about to go to the nurse's station, the sound of the toilet flushing stops me in my tracks. Turning in the direction of the bathroom, I let out a relieved exhale when Rose slowly comes out of the bathroom, a nurse in tow.

As if she can see the distress on my face, Rose frowns. "I'm sorry, I had to pee." She's slow moving and wincing with almost every step.

"It's okay, you could've woken me," I tell her before pulling the covers back before she gets into the bed.

"I didn't want to wake you. Your snores were too cute," she teases as she slowly slides into bed.

"I do not snore," I scoff.

"Tell him, Angie, he snores," she says, looking at the nurse who is hooking her monitors back up. To which, Angie nods her head and then laughs.

I shake my head and cover Rose back up once she gets settled. Leaning down, I kiss her lips softly, and Angie gags from behind me.

"I'll let you two lovebirds be," she teases before looking at Rose. "I'll be back with your meds in a few hours, missy."

It honestly doesn't surprise me that Rose has made friends with the staff. She has been taking this well, and I'm not sure if that's a good thing, or if I should be concerned. Her therapist agreed to do telehealth until she was well enough to come to the office, so hopefully once we get home and settled, she can start back with the sessions.

"Knock, knock," a voice says as they open the door.

"Hi Dr. Adams," Rose muses as he comes in.

"How are we feeling?" he asks, looking at her chart.

"I'm good. The pain is manageable. Nothing unbearable... unless I cough, that's pretty nasty," she tells him, picking at her fingers.

"Well, that's good," he says before coming over to examine her. He checks her incision sites from the splenectomy and her wounds that were sewn up. "As long as you have the proper care at home, and you take it easy... you can leave as soon as we get your prescriptions and your discharge paperwork." Rose's face lights up like a Christmas tree, and she gives him the biggest smile.

When the nurse comes in to help Rose change, I slip out of the room and go to the nurse's desk, asking them to get a message to the doctor, in hopes that he sees it before we leave. But to my surprise, he is coming out of another patient room. I flag him down, and ask the few questions I had to ask, and then thank him before returning to Rose's room.

After the nurse comes back with her medications and discharge instructions, she wheels Rose down to the entrance of the hospital while I bring the car around. Once she is settled in the car and ready to go, I reach over and grab Rose's hand.

"I cannot wait to get home and take a shower," Rose says as she leans her head back against the seat.

"I can't wait to sleep in my bed," I say with a laugh.

"I'm sorry you had to sleep in the uncomfortable chairs for two days," she says with a frown.

"I would have slept on the floor as long as I was with you," I say honestly, and she rolls her eyes with a smile.

With some music softly playing in the background, we head home. As we near the house, Rose squeezes my hand softly.

"It's okay. I'm not going to let anything happen to you," I promise her as we pull into the driveway.

"I just... I'm afraid to go inside. Is it still a mess?" she asks.

"No, Trevor and Amelia came and cleaned it up for us," I tell her after shaking my head.

"We owe them big time," she says with a nod. "I'll have to cook something."

"In a week or two when you can move around better, sure," I say as I get out of the car. Going to her side, I open her door and help her out. Slowly, we make our way up the front steps, and I open the door for her, but she freezes. At her hesitation, I take the step inside, and then turn around to her, reaching my hand out for her. She stares at my hand for a moment, chewing on her bottom lip, before she finally takes it and allows me to lead her inside.

Chapter Thirty-Two

Rosalind

I never really thought much about how it would feel to be back in the house. Wishing I had been better prepared, I slowly move from the living room to the kitchen. Atticus sits my medication on the counter and then turns to look at me.

"Do you want to go ahead and shower?" he asks.

While he's speaking, my eyes scan the room, and then come to rest on the spot on the floor where I dropped my mug. I can't get that memory out of my head. The fear that coursed through my veins when I saw Derek standing there. Sure, I'd had some self-defense training, but it wasn't as extensive as I'd needed to deal with him.

I can feel my breathing becoming shallow and my heart begins to race. Reaching forward, I grip the back of the kitchen chair and try to take deep breaths. That was a mistake. Taking a deep breath with broken ribs seems basically impossible, which causes me to panic even more.

Sensing my distress, Atticus is in front of me within seconds. "Hey, hey," he says softly, bending down so that I can see his eyes. "Eyes on me, baby," he whispers as he cups my cheek. "He's not here. He can't hurt you anymore."

Looking into his eyes, I take a breath as deep as I can without wanting to cry out in pain before repeating, "He's not here. He can't hurt me."

"That's it. You're doing a great job, baby," Atticus says encouragingly.

I close my eyes for a moment, and then reopen them, giving him a slight nod. "I would like to take my shower now, if that's okay."

"Come on," he says and takes my hand again, leading me to the bathroom.

When we step inside, I can feel him stiffen beside me momentarily. I realize that he hasn't been back home since the incident either. I can only imagine the torture he's going through. At least I don't remember a lot of it. Turning to face him, I give his hand a reassuring squeeze. He leans in and kisses my cheek before he pulls away.

"I forgot to grab the saran wrap to put around your cast, so it doesn't get wet. I'll be right back," he says before he rushes out of the room to grab the supplies.

Slowly making my way over to the shower, I reach in and turn the water on. Just as I do, Atticus comes in and sits the saran wrap and tape on the counter.

"Alright, let's get this baby wrapped up," he says as he motions for me to come over to him.

After my arm is nice and sealed off, he helps me undress and climb into the shower. Turning around, I'm surprised to see him stripped and climbing in the shower behind me. The shock must be evident on my face, because he steps closer to me and smirks.

"What? You thought I was going to let you shower on your own?" he teases. "You know me better than that, baby," he says before reaching over and grabbing the shampoo.

When he starts to wash my hair, the sensation of his fingers massaging my scalp gently causes me to moan softly.

"Don't do that," Atticus grits out before clearing his throat.

"Don't do what?" I ask with a raised eyebrow.

"Don't make those noises when right now, I can't do a damn thing about what it does to me." He stops massaging my hair and puts two of his fingers under my chin, lifting it up so he can rinse the soap from my hair.

Closing my eyes, I smile sheepishly at his words and bite my lip. "I apologize greatly."

He leans down and kisses my lips gently, and then grabs the loofa from behind me. Right before it touches my skin, I flinch instinctively, trying to brace myself for the pain.

"I'll be gentle, baby," he softly promises as he begins washing my body lightly.

My eyes close involuntarily and I lean my head against the shower wall. He wasn't lying, his touch is so gentle. Like he's afraid if he presses too hard, I'll shatter like glass. He grabs the shower head and brings it down to wash the soap off of me, before putting it back on the wall.

After he's done, he moves me to where I can sit on the bench that is built into the shower, and then begins to wash himself off. Chewing on my lip, I lean my head back and smirk as my eyes travel along his body. *Damn, am I lucky or what? Stop that Rose, this is not the time to be thinking of things like that. You can't even shower yourself.* I internally scold myself.

Atticus clears his throat, and my eyes snap up to his. He has a smirk on his face, and I feel my cheeks flush. He caught me red-handed ogling him. "Are you ready to get out, or do I need to run you a cold shower?" he teases before shutting the water off.

"I mean, from the looks of it, you could also benefit from a cold shower." His eyebrows raise again, and he lets out a laugh.

"I love you," he says between laughs, while he reaches out to grab the towel hanging from the hook.

He helps me dry off and then wraps the towel around me before following me to the bedroom. Digging through the drawers, he finds a pair of my underwear and then grabs one of his t-shirts and comes over to help me dress.

"I feel like a child," I whine.

"Doctor's orders. You need help until you're a little more stable on your feet." he shrugs.

Once I'm dressed, I walk over to the bed and frown. Laying down with broken ribs is not the most comfortable thing. Seeing me eye the bed, Atticus gives me a reassuring smile before he goes into the closet and comes back with a wedge pillow.

"The Dr. told me that you would need one of these to sleep comfortably, so I had Trevor grab one," he says with a sheepish smile.

"I could kiss you right now," I say excitedly.

"Who said you couldn't?" he asks as he walks over to me and carefully slips his arm around my waist, before leaning down and pressing his lips to mine.

Smiling into the kiss, I place my uninjured hand on his cheek, and pull back looking into his eyes, "As much as I would love to spend all night doing that," I say, "I think we both need a good night's rest."

He reluctantly agrees before sitting my wedge pillow on the bed and helping me lie down. "I'll go grab your meds, give me just a second," he says before he throws on a pair of sweatpants and disappears from the room to go get them.

I didn't realize how tired I was until I got settled in the bed, but now I'm having trouble keeping my eyes open. Just as I'm about to drift off to sleep, my phone vibrates on the nightstand and I reach for it, careful not to hurt my ribs. Opening the notification, it's a link to a news article from Amelia.

The headline makes my jaw drop, and I yell for Atticus, "Attie! Come here!"

I look up as he comes running, "What? Are you okay?" he asks, looking me over frantically.

"I'm fine. Look at this," I say, thrusting the phone in his face.

As he reads it, his eyes grow wide and bite my lip. "I didn't want this to happen," I say, taking my phone back and reading the headline one more time. "I just wanted him to answer for his crimes."

Collegiate Athlete, Derek Murphy, Killed in Drunk Driving Accident.

I feel tears welling in my eyes, and Atticus reaches over, rubbing my thigh, "It's over baby," he whispers softly before pulling me to him.

According to the article, Derek had been drinking and thought it'd be a good idea to take his car for a joy ride. It's been raining for a few days now and he hydroplaned and wrapped his car around a tree. He was DOA.

It's over. I can't believe it.

Chapter Thirty-Three

Atticus

The next four weeks go by rather quickly. Rosalind's father came, apologizing several times that he couldn't come as soon as I called, and stayed for a week before he had to head back home for work. He promised he would be back soon, and I made sure to let him know he was always welcome. Her mother, on the other hand, dropped by for a total of twenty minutes two weeks after she had been home, told her she looked rough, and we haven't heard anything else from her. I'm not so sure Rose is even upset about that.

Derek still haunts Rose's dreams, and sometimes I catch her looking over her shoulder like he's going to be standing there waiting for her. Her therapy has started back on a regular schedule, her wounds are healing nicely, and her cast came off last week. The doctor expects her ribs to be healed within the next two weeks.

It's getting easier to walk in the bathroom and not relive that moment my world almost stopped. For the first week, I could barely bring myself to go in there without her. I needed her by my side just to remind me that she was okay.

I'm sitting in the living room when she walks in from a nap. "Good afternoon, babe," I say as she walks over and sits on my lap.

"Mm, afternoon," she murmurs before placing her head on my shoulder.

"I have a surprise for you," I whisper in her ear, causing her to sit upright again.

"Oooh, what is it?" she asks excitedly.

"If I told you, it wouldn't be a surprise," I say, reaching up to brush a strand of hair out of her face. "I already have everything set up, so I just need you to go get dressed. Wear comfy clothing."

She jumps up off my lap, wincing a little at the discomfort in her ribs, before taking off to the bedroom. I chuckle as I walk to the hall closet and pull out our overnight bags I packed while she was napping. While she's changing, I hurry and put them in the back of the car before she notices. I'm just walking back in the house when she walks out of the bedroom in a pair of leggings and my hoodie.

"Have I told you how much I love it when you wear that hoodie?" I ask as I slip my arms around her waist, pulling her closer.

"Almost every single time I wear it," she muses before standing on her tiptoes and pressing her lips against mine.

Reluctantly, I pull away and look down at her. "We better get going."

After setting the alarm, we head out to the car. She immediately turns her music on and begins to sing along. I glance at her out of the corner of my eye several times during the drive. The carefree smile she has on her face is breathtaking.

As I take a familiar exit, she sits up in the seat and looks over at me. "We're going to the cabin!" she says with a grin.

"Yes, we are, honey," I tell her with a smile. "I figured we could use a nice little getaway."

She doesn't stop smiling the rest of the trip. I was hoping to be able to bring her out here before the snow stopped, but unfortunately, I wasn't able to. I know it doesn't matter to her when we come though, because she loves being here all the time.

As I pull into the driveway and put the car in park, she unbuckles and squeals excitedly. "Do you know what the first thing I'm going to do is?" she asks with a smile. "I'm getting in that damn hot tub."

Chuckling to myself, I hand her the keys for the door while I grab our bags. "That sounds like a great idea, baby."

Once inside, she practically sprints to the bedroom. I walk out to the hot tub and turn it on so that it will be ready for us after we change. Then I head inside to grab my trunks and stop in my tracks. She's standing naked at the foot of the bed with her back to me. I've seen her naked before, but these last couple of weeks have about done me in. Just as I go to tear my eyes away from her ass, she turns and this time she catches me. I give her a wink and stride over to the drawer, pulling out my trunks.

After we both have changed, Rose grabs my hand and drags me downstairs. When we get to the hot tub, I remove the cover and help her inside. She moans softly as she sinks down into the warm water. Cursing under my breath, I lean my head back, looking up at the sky before climbing in.

Rose instantly slides over to me once I'm situated, and I put my arm around her shoulders. We sit in silence for the better part of an hour, just relaxing and being content with each other's company. It's been a while since we have been able to relax and simply not worry about what's coming.

I have my head leaned back and my eyes closed when Rose moves from under my arm and into my lap. She puts her arms around my neck and leans down, closing the distance between us before pressing her lips to mine. My hand immediately goes to the back of her head, deepening the kiss, and the other slides around her hip, pulling her flush against me. Pulling away, she kisses down to my neck. Leaning my head to the side, I let out a soft groan.

"Don't start something you can't finish, honey." I warn.

"Who said I can't finish?" she asks with an eyebrow raised in challenge.

This woman is trying to kill me.

Chapter Thirty-Four

Rosalind

As soon as I started kissing Atticus on the neck, I knew I was playing with fire. The tension has been growing between us for the last few weeks, and it's driving me crazy. He told me that he isn't going to make the first move, and that he wanted me to initiate the first time we have any sort of intimacy other than kissing. I love him for that. He's trying to give me control since I still freak out sometimes when we touch. It's not as bad anymore, though, and I am ready to move on.

After a few minutes of heavy kissing, I stand and climb out of the hot tub before drying off. I saunter to the door and look back at him over my shoulder before motioning for him to follow me. He climbs out so fast I think he's going to slip and fall. It causes me to giggle as I take off to the bedroom.

As I walk, I strip out of my bathing suit, leaving a trail behind me, and I hear him cursing. Smirking to myself, I climb on the bed just as he bursts through the door. Shutting the door behind him, he walks over to the bed and discards his trunks before joining me. Careful not to put pressure on my ribs, he hovers over me as his hand finds mine, pinning it above my head. He leans down to kiss me gently before pulling away.

"Are you sure?" he asks, and I nod. "Words, baby. I need words."

"I'm sure, Atticus," I breathe out, "Now stop talking."

The next morning, I wake wrapped in Atticus's arms. He's still snoring softly, and I stifle a laugh. *He doesn't snore my ass.* After much effort,

I manage to slip out of his arms and tiptoe to the bathroom. Thinking back to last night, I smile to myself. All of that sexual tension that had been building finally exploded. My body is sore, but for all the right reasons this time.

Sliding on one of Atticus's t-shirts, I head to the kitchen, making myself a cup of coffee and sitting at the kitchen table. Just as I finish my coffee, the sound of Atticus's footsteps draws my attention to the stairs.

"Morning, honey," he says, his voice husky.

"Good morning!" I reply as I lean up, and he kisses my cheek, while grabbing my mug to refill it.

"How are you feeling this morning?" Pouring himself a cup of coffee, he turns to look at me, waiting on my reply.

"I'm a little sore," I answer honestly. "But nothing some ibuprofen won't fix."

He nods and sits my mug down in front of me before sitting in the seat beside me. "What do you want to do today?" he asks before taking a sip of his coffee.

"Well, I was thinking of having a movie marathon." I reply, blowing on my hot coffee.

"That sounds great," he says with a smile.

Later that afternoon, we are cuddled up on the couch in the theater room, watching 'Grownups'. Atticus has his arm around me, and I'm leaned against him with my hand resting on his thigh. After the movie ends, Atticus turns my chin toward him, and I give him a small smile.

"I love you, Rosalind," he whispers, before leaning down to kiss me deeply.

Without breaking the kiss, I straddle him and wrap my arms around his neck. His hand trails down my back and slips under the hem of my shirt. His soft touch causes shivers to run down my spine. Grinning against my lips, the other hand tangles in my hair, deepening the kiss. He grabs the hem of my shirt and lifts it up over my head before discarding it on the floor. Moving his hands to my ass, he holds me against him as he stands. He then proceeds to lay me down on the couch. His lips trailing down my neck cause a soft moan to escape my lips.

This is going to be a tiring weekend.

When Monday comes, I'm disappointed that we have to return to the real world. It was nice being in our own little bubble for the weekend, without any responsibilities. Atticus has classes, and I received a pass for the time I was off, but I still have to do work to make up for what I missed.

"I need a vacation from this vacation," I tease as I look over at him while he drives.

"Tell me about it. My girlfriend couldn't keep her hands off me and I am exhausted," he teases, before grabbing my hand and kissing the back of it. We continue our drive home singing along with the music, and talking about what the week will hold.

Pulling into the house, I'm surprised to find Amelia and Trevor waiting on the porch. Getting out, I rush up to Amelia and give her a hug. She hugs me back, careful not to put too much pressure on my ribs.

"We are sorry to just barge in," Amelia says excitedly, "but I needed to show you this." She says as she holds her hand out to me, revealing a shiny diamond ring.

"Oh my gosh!" I scream and give her another hug, ignoring the pain in my side. "Damn Trev," I say as I inspect the ring, "you picked a nice one."

"Isn't it beautiful?" Amelia gushes.

"Congratulations, man," Atticus says from beside me as he rests his arm across my shoulders.

"Now it's your turn," Trevor teases as he winks at me.

I laugh and glance at Atticus. "Eventually." Atticus and I haven't exactly had a chance to talk about marriage. Yes, we have been friends for two years. However, I'm still in the early stages of healing mentally from all that has happened in the last few months.

As the men talk, Amelia pulls me to the side to discuss wedding details. Apparently, Trevor proposed Friday night, and she has spent all weekend planning out her perfect wedding. We make plans to go dress shopping next weekend so she can get a feel for the style she is looking for.

When Trevor and Amelia leave, we head inside and Atticus gets ready for class, and I get ready for my first in person therapy session since I got out of the hospital. Walking out to the car, I turn to face Atticus, who is staring at me with worry.

"I will be fine, honey," I say softly, reaching up to cup his cheek. "He can't hurt me anymore."

"I know, but I just don't want to leave you." He sighs.

"Attie," I say, leaning up to kiss him, "you have to let me do things on my own sometimes. It's not healthy for us to be so dependent on one another."

He considers my words before giving me a nod. "You're right, but that doesn't mean I have to like it."

"I'll be here after your class." I promise, "I love you," I add before getting in my car and making my way to my therapist's office.

Chapter Thirty-Five

Atticus

Just as I'm pulling into the school parking lot, I get a text from Rose telling me she made it to her appointment. I shoot her a quick reply and then grab my books heading into class. Fidgeting with my pencil while waiting to be dismissed, I receive another text. This time it's from Coach.

Come see me after class.

Raising my eyebrow, I lock my phone and put it in my pocket before the professor catches me. I'm not sure what he wants from me, considering the season is over. I didn't get to play ninety percent of the season because of Derek.

After class, I head to the gym and find Coach in his office.

"Reed," he greets me. "Have a seat."

I do as he says and take the seat in front of his desk. "You wanted to see me?"

"It seems I owe you an apology." He looks down at his desk before looking back up at me. "I regret not considering your side of the story, and I'm sorry for depriving you of an entire season of basketball."

"Thank you, Coach," I say with a nod.

He gives me an apologetic smile. "I also want to apologize for insinuating that whatever you were fighting over wasn't worth it. I should've known something was up because in the years I've known you, you have never reacted that way, even though you've had plenty of times to do so."

"I told you that day that it was worth everything and more," I say, "and I stand by what I said. I'd do it again in a heartbeat. If there's anything I would do differently, it would be going straight home after the scrimmage instead of showering."

"Son, you can't beat yourself up over that," he says as he leans forward, resting his clasped hands on his desk.

"I know, and I will have to forgive myself eventually. But right now, I can't," I say as I look down at my hands.

"I haven't met Rose. I've only seen her at ballgames. But I doubt she blames you for what happened." Coach leans back in his chair and looks at his watch. "I guess you better get going. Your next class starts in ten minutes."

Nodding, I stand from the chair and begin to leave, but I stop and turn back around. "Hey Coach..." I say, propping my hand on the door frame. "Thank you for everything you've done for me. It's been hard without my dad around, and you made it a little easier," I say before giving him a nod and heading to class.

I'm anxious to get home to Rose, so as soon as I'm dismissed from my last class, I practically sprint to my Jeep. After I talked with Coach, I decided that I was going to talk to her about that night, not necessarily about the attack, but about how I should've been there and the guilt I've been carrying over it.

After pulling into the driveway, I put the car in park and then take a deep breath. I head inside and as soon as I walk in, the smell of burgers consumes me, making my mouth water. I find Rose in the kitchen, standing at the stove and making dinner.

"Hey honey," she says as she hears me throw my keys on the counter.

"Hey babe." I walk over to give her a kiss on the head before looking down at the food. "Dinner smells amazing."

"Thank you." She blushes.

"How was therapy?" I slide my arms around her waist.

"It was really good. Misty is pleased with my progress." She turns the stove off and faces me. "What's wrong?" she asks, her eyes searching my face.

"Can we sit down and talk before we eat?" I ask, looking away from her.

"Atticus are you going to break up with me?" she asks.

My eyebrows furrow and I shake my head. "No woman, I just want to talk to you about something." I grab her hand and lead her over to the kitchen table, sitting down with her. "I talked with Coach today, and he apologized for kicking me off the team without doing any digging. He also told me that I can't keep blaming myself."

Rose scrunches her face up in confusion. "What do you mean, blaming yourself?"

"I have been beating myself up since I found out about what happened. I should have just showered at home and walked you to your car." My hands reach across to grab hers. "If I had been with you, I could have prevented this whole thing."

"Baby," Rose says with a frown. "You didn't know what was going to happen. No one did. You can't blame yourself for this. The only person who is at fault is Derek. It never even crossed my mind that you were at fault."

Her words seem to lift a thousand pounds off my shoulders, and I squeeze her hand gently. "Thank you," I whisper softly before leaning over and kissing her.

"I love you, Atticus Michael." She reaches up and cups my cheek.

I smile as I peck her lips one more time before getting up. "I love you too, Rosalind."

Chapter Thirty-Six

Rosalind

Hearing Atticus admit that he has been beating himself up over not being there for me that night absolutely breaks my heart. I never once even considered blaming him, and even if there was a reason to blame him, I wouldn't. He would never let anything bad happen to me if he could help it.

I lean forward and press a soft kiss to his lips before looking into his eyes. "You need to forgive yourself, Atticus."

He looks down at his hands and sighs.

"Come on, let's eat," I say as I get up and make my way back to the stove. I make both of our plates before bringing them back over to the table and sitting his plate in front of him. "Do you want water?"

"Yes, please," he mumbles softly.

Grabbing two waters, I join him at the table. We eat silently, except for Atticus complimenting my burger. I steal a few glances of him while we eat. I really hope he forgives himself. I know what it's like to hold on to the guilt over something you can't control. It will eat him alive.

Once we finish dinner, Atticus tells me to go take a bath while he does the dishes. I give him a kiss on the cheek and head to the bathroom, before turning on the bath and filling it up with water and bubble bath. After I undress, I climb in, sinking into the warm water and letting out a content sigh. I let my eyes close as I relax in the tub, but they quickly reopen when I hear the door to the bathroom open.

"Attie, are you okay?" I ask as I take in his concerned appearance.

"*Fuck*," he curses. "I thought I was over this."

"Over what?" I ask, sitting up and turning to face him.

"The whole, you in the bathroom alone thing. I know it's clingy and I know I'm probably getting on your nerves," he says with a sigh. "I just can't help it. Every time I'm afraid I will walk in and find you like that again."

Pulling the stopper to let the water drain out, I grab my towel and wrap it around my body before walking over to him. "Listen to me," I say softly, "I have been there. I still have moments where it's hard not to freak out. But I will never tell you that you're getting on my nerves for worrying about me."

He wraps his arms around me and pulls me close. "I have never been so scared in my life. When I saw you lying there on the floor, Rosalind, I thought that I had lost you forever."

"I know, baby. I know. But you didn't. I'm still here," I murmur as I lay my head on his chest. "I promised you I wouldn't leave you again, didn't I?"

His hand runs through my hair as we stand there while he holds me. I close my eyes against his chest and exhale softly. My hands slide around his waist, and I rub his back gently.

"I'm sorry, Rose. I don't mean to take what happened to you and turn it around to be about me," Atticus says while kissing the top of my head.

"Don't do that." I grip his chin lightly, making him look at me. "You experienced something traumatic too, Atticus. I can't imagine what kind of mess I would be if the roles were reversed, and I had found you."

Resting his forehead on mine, he closes his eyes and brings both hands up to cup my cheeks. "I don't know how I got so lucky to have someone like you, but I'm going to spend every day making sure you know how much I cherish you."

Smiling up at him, I place my hands over his and close the distance between our lips. "I guess we are both pretty lucky." I say before pulling away and grabbing his hand. "Let's go to bed, baby. It's been a long day."

He leads me to the bed and climbs in before holding the covers back so I can slide in and cuddle up to him. Once I'm settled in, his hand goes around my waist and holds me against him. Slowly, I find myself drifting off to sleep.

"Good night, Rose." Atticus whispers in my ear, right before sleep takes over.

The next morning, I wake to my phone ringing. Atticus groans beside me, covering his head with his pillow. I chuckle while grabbing my phone. It's the school. When I answer it, I'm surprised to hear that it is the new dean. She tells me that the reason behind her call is to invite me back to in person classes for next semester.

I thank her for the offer and tell her that I will get back to her in a few days. Although I miss being in person, I'm not sure I want to go and be reminded of Derek everywhere I turn. Although he is dead, and I know he can't hurt me anymore, his memory still haunts me.

Atticus has mentioned us packing up and moving to somewhere several times, other than Trevor and Amelia, we have nothing holding us here anymore. I've entertained the idea a few times. I just don't know if there's anywhere I can go that will rid me of Derek. I've been unpacking that in therapy as well. What happened to him was not my fault, and I don't need to feel guilty about it. Yet somehow, I still do.

Putting my phone back on the nightstand, Atticus rolls over and envelops me in his arms again. "We need to make a rule that phones go on 'do not disturb' when we are sleeping and we can't turn them back on until we get out of bed." He grumbles.

I snuggle into his chest and laugh softly. "Although that sounds amazing, that is not practical. What if Trevor or Amelia need us?"

"I hate it when you're right," Atticus says with a heavy sigh.

Smiling, I wiggle out of his embrace and saunter to the bathroom. "Would you like to join me in the shower?" I call over my shoulder.

"If I ever say no to that, then I need to go to the doctor," Atticus replies, jumping out of bed.

Chapter Thirty-Seven

Atticus

After our shower, I'm standing in the bedroom when my phone goes off. Grabbing it to check the notification, I smile when I see that it is from Rose's dad. When he came to visit after Rose got out of the hospital, he and I bonded over several topics. Sports was a big one that we talked about for hours while Rose just sat and enjoyed her 'two favorite men', her words, not mine, getting along. I had sent him a message yesterday about us coming to see him this week and he just replied, saying his schedule was clear. I had promised Rose that we would go see him more often.

Quickly pulling up flights, I find one departing this evening that will have us arriving at her dad's late tonight. Just as I finish checking out, I walk into the bathroom where Rose is blow drying her hair. She looks over at me with a raised eyebrow. "What are you so smiley for?"

"After I get out of class, I'm taking you somewhere," I reply. "So you better have your bag packed when we get home."

She eyes me curiously, and I wink at her before leaving the bathroom to get ready. Once I'm dressed, I throw some clothes in a bag and sit it by the door. I grab her bag out of the closet and put it on the bed for her before going back to the bathroom.

"Your bag is on the bed. I have to run, but I will be back to get you after class. I love you," I say as I lean down, pecking her lips gently and then walking out of the bathroom. When I get in the car, I send her dad a text back, letting him know that we will be getting in late tonight and will stay in a hotel until he gets up. Then I head to class.

This is pointless. I think to myself as the professor drones on and on. Just as I'm about to get up and leave, the professor dismisses us and I'm out the door in seconds. Once I arrive at the house, I get out and head inside. "Rose, I'm home. Are you ready to go?" I call out as I walk to the bedroom.

"Yeah, I'm all ready!" she says as she turns around to greet me with a smile.

"Let's get going then. Our plane departs in two hours," I inform her before grabbing her bag off the bed.

"Plane?" she questions, following me out of the bedroom to the car.

"Yes, honey." I throw our bags into the trunk and set the security system on my phone.

She eyes me suspiciously, but as I start driving toward the airport, I hand her my phone with the ticket information pulled up. I glance over at her as it registers, and she breaks out into a huge smile.

"Thank you, Atticus." Her hand reaches over to find mine, and I lace our fingers together.

"Anything for you," I say, bringing her hand to my lips and kissing the back.

We make it to the airport and through security right when they call our flight for boarding. Making it to the terminal just in time, we board and find our seats. Without hesitation, I tell her to take the window seat. She gives me a grin before sliding into her seat. I sit down beside her and take her hand in mine.

We buckle up when the fasten seatbelt sign comes on and the pilot announces our departure. I glance over at Rose, who is staring out the window, mesmerized by the lights flying by. When she turns back to look at me and catches me staring at her, she gives me a wink and then leans up, kissing me softly.

We watch an inflight movie to pass the time, but before we know it, the seatbelt sign comes back on, and we are landing. When we are cleared to exit the plane, I grab our bags in one hand and take Rose's with my other. We flag down a taxi, and I give them the directions to our hotel.

"We are staying in a hotel tonight and then at your dads for the rest of the trip. I just didn't want to bother him coming in late," I explain whenever I see Rose's questioning look.

She nods in understanding and then looks out the window, watching the city buzz by. After tipping the cab driver, I hold the door open for Rose, and we make our way into the hotel. I've booked a suite for us, even though it's only for tonight. I know she will be tired from traveling, but I figured she wouldn't pass up a jacuzzi room.

When we walk in, she immediately turns to look at me and smiles. *Great call on the room.* She stops short of the jacuzzi and turns to face me as I shut the door. "I seriously didn't bring a suit this time," she says with a frown while I sit our bags down on the bed.

Unzipping mine, I pull out her bathing suit and my trunks. "I brought them, orrr..." I say, dragging out the 'r.' "We can just go with no suit."

"Oh, scandalous," she teases as she strips out of her clothes. "I think I'll skip the skinny dipping for now." Grabbing the suit out of my hand, she slides it on and then gets in.

"Aw man, it was worth a shot," I playfully pout before changing and climb in after her.

I pull her into my lap with her back pressed against my chest, and she leans her head back, resting it on my shoulder. She lets out a soft exhale and slides her hands into mine, resting our joined hands in her lap. We sit in comfortable silence for close to half an hour.

"You know," I say breaking the silence and resting my head against hers. "I was thinking if you wanted to transfer to another school, we could think about coming here?"

"I don't know, Attie," she says, chewing on her lip. "Tennessee is my home. It will be hard to leave it."

"It's just a suggestion. We can live wherever you want, honey." My hands squeeze hers gently.

A few moments of quiet silence go by before I look over at the clock on the nightstand, "As much as I'd like to spend all night here, your dad said that he would be by to get us for breakfast first thing in the morning."

"He was always a big breakfast person," she says with a laugh, before standing up and getting out.

Following behind her, I grab the string to her bathing suit top, tugging gently and smirking when it comes undone. Brushing her hair to the side, I lean down and pepper her neck in kisses. Rose lets out a soft moan and I grin against her skin.

Pulling away, I grab a towel and dry off before discarding my trunks. I dig through my bag for a pair of boxers and slide them on before climbing into the bed. Rose joins me once she throws on her pajamas and takes her usual place against my chest.

"I love you," she whispers with a yawn.

"I love you too, honey," I reply and tighten my grip on her before we both drift off to sleep.

Chapter Thirty-Eight

Rosalind

Atticus surprising me with a trip to my dad's was just what I needed this weekend. Although with the way he and my dad have been getting along since we got here, he could've just left me at home. I don't mind playing the third wheel as long as they're getting along. This extended weekend has been a breath of fresh air. Sure, going to the cabin is a great getaway, but this is different.

It's the final day with my dad and we are eating at a nice little Italian restaurant, and Atticus and my dad are both rambling on about some basketball team. To be honest, I haven't been paying attention. I've been busy daydreaming about the possibilities of living here. Is Atticus onto something? Would I be happier here? I know he says he's happy wherever I am, but I want to make sure he's genuinely happy.

Snapping me out of my trance, Atticus reaches over and takes my hand. "You okay there, Rose?" he asks with a raised eyebrow.

"Yeah, I'm good. I was just thinking about how nice this trip has been," I reply before taking a sip of my water.

"I was just telling your dad here that we were going to have to come out again," he says and my dad chuckles.

"Yeah, it will be nice to have you guys here from time to time," my dad says with a nod.

"Well dad, maybe we will come out for an extended period over the summer?" I offer with a raised eyebrow.

"I would love that," my dad replies and reaches over, putting his hand on mine and squeezing gently. "I'm so glad that you are doing better."

"Me too, dad," I reply, giving him a small smile.

After dinner, my dad drops us off at the airport, promising to come visit soon. We board our flight and begin our journey home. I let out a content sigh as our plane lands back in Tennessee and we make our way to the car.

"It's nice to go on vacations," I say as I get in the car, "but I also love being home."

"I agree." Atticus nods before driving out of the airport parking lot.

The drive home is short, and by the time we crawl into bed, we are exhausted. The week ahead is full of classes, therapy, and I've told Atticus that I'm ready to get back to the gym. Even though the threat of Derek is gone, I will never allow myself to be so vulnerable that I'm in that position again. Atticus made me promise that I would take it easy during the first few sessions, which is fine with me. I'm just so happy to be getting back to it.

I fall asleep listening to Atticus's rhythmic snoring. Life couldn't get any better than this.

"Oh my goodness, I *love* that one," I gush as Amelia walks out in what feels like the twentieth wedding dress. This one accentuates her curves and best features perfectly. "Trevor is going to lose his mind!"

She looked at me through the mirror, tears shining in her eyes. "I think this is it!"

After she changes, she comes out and shoves me in the direction of the fitting room one of the attendants stacked with dresses for my maid of honor dress. Laughing, I step inside and look through the dresses. They're pretty, but one of them I keep coming back to.

"Hey Amelia, what happens if I just can't stop looking at one?" I yell out to her.

"Try it on! I'm dying out here." Amelia claps her hands in a 'get a move on,' way.

I take off my clothes and then slip on the dress. When I walk out of the fitting room, Amelia's jaw drops.

"*Damn*, bitch," she whistles. "I don't know if you can wear that to my wedding. Something about upstaging the bride just doesn't sound right."

"Stop it," I say and roll my eyes before turning to the mirror. The sight before me makes me understand why Amelia's jaw dropped. The dress is a satin dusty blue color with a deep V-neck and a slit that begins a few inches above my knee.

"Atticus is going to have a heart attack when he sees you in that," she says as she comes over to stand beside me.

"You like it? This is your wedding. Is this what you want?" I ask, looking over at her.

"It's perfect." With a nod, Amelia tells the attendant that we'll take it.

Once I'm changed and we have paid for the dresses, Amelia and I turn the rest of the day into a spa day. By the time I return home, I'm ready to curl up on the couch and watch a movie with Atticus.

"Hey, Attie. I'm home," I say, walking through the front door before locking it behind me.

"Hello, gorgeous," Atticus calls from the kitchen. "I made your favorite dinner. Come look."

"I can tell. It smells so good in here." Walking into the kitchen, I smile as Atticus is taking the meatloaf out of the oven.

"How was your day with Amelia?" he asks as he leans over and kisses my cheek.

"It was great. She found her wedding dress, and we found my dress, too." At the mention of my dress, his interest piques.

"Oh yeah? What's your dress look like?" he questions.

"It's a dusty blue color, with a deep V-neck that comes to about right here," I say, pointing to a spot right under my breastbone. "A slit that starts here." I point to a spot above my knee. "Oh, and it's satin," I add.

"God, you're going to kill me," he groans.

I giggle and grab two plates, then begin plating our food. He has gone all out with this meal, making all my favorites. Meatloaf, mashed potatoes, green beans, and mac and cheese. I eye him suspiciously. "What's going on? Why have you made my favorite meal?"

"I just like to spoil you, baby," he says and grabs our plates, walking over to the kitchen table. "Can't I do that?"

"I mean, yeah, you can..." I say as I sit down.

"Good," he muses with a smile. "Oh, I meant to tell you," he says after taking a bite of his food. "Coach asked me to come back next season."

"That's awesome! What did you tell him?" Taking a drink of my water, I continue eating, but stop when I hear the words that come out of his mouth.

"I told him thanks, but I was going to have to pass on the offer," he says, avoiding my stare.

"Atticus..." I start, but he cuts me off.

"I thought about it, honestly," he assures me. "It's just... I don't know. I love basketball, don't get me wrong. But, I was kicked off the team, and the world kept spinning. It didn't stop like I always thought it would if I couldn't play. I'm staying in shape thanks to Brandon and the guys at the gym. I'm just happier without it."

"You know I'll support you no matter what," I say, reaching over to grab his hand. "I just want to make sure that you're sure."

"I'm sure, baby. I don't need it anymore," he tells me as he squeezes my hand. "I have everything I could ever need."

Chapter Thirty-Nine

Rosalind

Seven Months Later

"Rosalind, are you even paying attention to the game?" Amelia asks as she glares at me.

"Yeah, sorry, I was just seeing where Atticus was. He should be here by now," I say, putting my phone away and sliding it into my back pocket.

"I'm sure he's around here somewhere," she says as she glances around. She's acting weirder than normal, and I don't know if it's the pregnancy hormones, or what, but I like the new Amelia.

She and Trevor got married four months ago and wasted no time in starting a family. In Amelia's words, 'Trevor wants a big family', so they decided to start right away. Atticus has played around with the idea of kids, but I told him I wanted to wait until we got married and spent some time with just us.

My therapy has been going well, and last week made a full year since the night Derek attacked me. As awful as I thought the day would be, it actually wasn't that bad. Atticus, Trevor, and Amelia made sure that I was busy the entire day, and when it was time for bed, Atticus was there for the nightmares. They still visit to me, but not as often. Usually, I only have one or two a week, unless I'm stressed. Then they come with a vengeance.

"Hey baby, sorry I'm late," Atticus says as he appears at my side, snapping me out of my thoughts.

"It's okay, you just missed the entire first half," I say, propping my hands on my hips. "Where were you?"

"I was late leaving the gym. I was sparring with Brandon, and we lost track of time," he explains, and I laugh softly.

"I'm going to start sending Gabe text alerts when it's time for you to leave," I tease.

He chuckles and then turns his attention to the game. It's almost halftime and we are up by twenty. Just as the halftime buzzer sounds, Atticus kisses my cheek. "I'll be back. Coach wanted to see me at halftime."

"Okay, we will be here," I say before turning to Amelia, who is scarfing down some nachos. "Can the pregnant lady spare a nacho?"

"Yes, but only one." She holds the container out to me, and I laugh while taking one.

Just as I finish eating the nacho, the lights dim for the halftime show. "Oh, I love watching these."

Amelia just smirks at me while she digs out another nacho, "Yes, we know."

"We?" I question with a raised eyebrow, still looking at her.

"Rosalind Johnson." My name crackles over the loudspeaker, and I turn to look in confusion. My eyes go to half court, where Atticus is standing, a smile on his lips. When our eyes meet, he motions for me to join him. *Oh shit.*

"Rose, don't make me drag you out there," Amelia says beside me as she polishes off her nachos. Rolling my eyes at her, I laugh and then make my way to Atticus. Each step I take, I feel the nervous flutters going wild in my stomach.

When I stop in front of Atticus, I squint my eyes at him. "I thought Coach wanted to see you?"

He smiles at me and takes my hand. "Rosalind Olivia, you have been my best friend since the very first time we met. I remember that day like it was yesterday. Amelia was introducing you to Trevor, and I crashed the party. It was this very spot actually," he says, glancing down at the floor and then back at me.

My heart is flying a hundred miles per hour and I'm pretty sure my mouth is so dry I wouldn't be able to speak even if I wanted to.

"Somewhere in those two years of being inseparable, you slowly became my everything. We have been through hell and back this past year, but I'm so glad that you have been by my side. I promised myself that night I thought I was going to lose you, that if you came back to me, I would spend every waking moment of the rest of my life showing you just how much I loved you." He grabs something out of his pocket. "And as you know, I don't make promises I can't keep," he says as he kneels in front of me.

Oh my god. He's really doing it. My hand comes up to cover my mouth and I will the tears in my eyes to stay put.

"Rosalind Olivia Johnson, will you help me keep that promise and say yes to being my wife?" he asks, looking up at me with a hopeful expression.

I don't bother trying to speak. I just nod my head and wipe away the tears that betrayed me.

Relief visible on his face, he slides the beautiful round cut diamond ring on my finger. Then he stands and pulls me to him, pressing his lips to mine. The audience erupting into a cheer.

Breaking the kiss, I look into his eyes with a smile, "I love you, Atticus Michael."

"And I love you, Rosalind Olivia," he murmurs before kissing me one more time. "I think we better get out of the middle of the court so they can resume the game."

Walking off the floor, Amelia is waiting for us, practically bursting with excitement. "This has been the hardest secret to keep!" she gushes as she wraps her arms around me.

"I should've known something was up when you agreed to share your nachos." Atticus wraps his arms around me from behind and gives me a kiss on the cheek. "And you, mister," I say, turning to face him. "How did you pull this off so well? You are awful at keeping secrets."

"A lot of help," he says with a laugh. "When we went to your dad's seven months ago, I really did want you to see him, but I also had an ulterior motive. One night while you were in the shower, I asked his permission and told him my plan. I wanted to wait a few months because I didn't want to disrupt your healing, but you've been doing so well. I decided that now was the right time."

"Of course, I said yes," my dad says from behind me.

"Dad!" Throwing my arms around him, he wraps me in a bear hug. "Wow, Atticus, you really thought of everything!"

"I tried my best," he says sheepishly, rubbing the back of his neck.

We make our way back to our seats, and I look down at the ring on my hand. If you had told me a year ago that I would be standing here, engaged to Atticus, and healing from the trauma Derek caused, I would call you a liar.

When I look up at Atticus is already staring down at me. "Do you like your ring?" he asks with a smile.

"I love it so much, Attie," I reply and lean up on my tiptoes, giving him a quick kiss on the cheek.

Chapter Forty

Atticus

Two Years Later

Looking at myself in the mirror, I double check my tie and then turn to face Trevor. "Everything looks good?" I ask nervously as I fidget with the cuffs on my shirt.

"Everything looks good," he assures me, before checking his watch. "It's time."

I take one more glance at myself in the mirror before taking a deep breath and walking out of the room and to the gazebo. It's a new addition to the property that the cabin sits on, and made the perfect venue for our wedding.

The one condition to our engagement Rose laid out was that she wanted to wait until she graduated to get married. I agreed, and we set the date for the summer after graduation. We have decided to move closer to Rose's dad since we are there so often. Rose already has a job waiting for her as a kindergarten teacher, and I accepted the head basketball coach position at the local high school.

Trevor and I take our places at the altar, and the officiate joins us. Looking out at our friends and family, I find myself smiling. However, if we don't get this started soon, I might throw up. My nerves are all over the place. Turning, I look at Trevor and eye his pocket. "You have the rings, right?"

"Shit. I left them in the room." He pats his pocket before looking up at me.

"Trevor, this is not the time, man," I grumble out, and he laughs.

"I'm just messing with you. They're right here," he says.

Soon the music begins, and the doors open, revealing Willow, Amelia and Trevor's little girl. She just turned two and I swear she has Uncle At and Aunt Rose wrapped around her little finger. She bounds down the aisle with her little basket of flowers throwing clumps here and there.

I have to give the girl credit. She does a great job of staying on task. That is until she sees her daddy. Then it's game over. "Daddy!" she squeals as she darts down the last portion of the aisle and he bends down to scoop her up, laughing. Amelia exits the cabin after Willow, and makes her way down the aisle as well, giving me a wink when she takes her respective place across from Trevor.

The doors close and the music changes. *This is it.*

When the doors open to reveal Rose and her father, the smile that spreads across my face is indescribable. She is absolutely breathtaking. The tears begin to creep into my vision, and I quickly wipe them away, not wanting to miss a single moment.

Her dress is a simple white satin strapless A-line gown. Well, she called it simple, but there is nothing simple about this dress. It hugs her body in all the right places, and I swear she is glowing.

Rose comes to stand in front of me after her father gives her away. My hands are shaking as I take hers in mine, and she gives me a reassuring squeeze. It takes everything in me not to take her in my arms and kiss her right then.

The officiant begins the ceremony and when it comes time to say our vows, Rose gives me an encouraging smile. Clearing my throat, I look into her eyes. "Rosalind, from the very first time I laid eyes on you, I knew that you were going to be an important person in my life. I just underestimated how important. I always say I don't know how I got lucky enough to call you mine, but I plan on spending the rest of my life cherishing every moment spent together."

Rose is looking up at me with eyes full of tears and a huge smile on her face. "I promise to love you fiercely and unconditionally, just as you deserve for the rest of our lives. I promise that no matter what life throws at us, you will find me standing by your side, fighting through it all. You are the absolute love of my life, and I will love you until the end of time."

"Wow," Rose begins, "That's going to be a tough act to follow." She gives me a smile before continuing. "Atticus, when we first met, I thought that you came into my life just when I needed you most. I didn't realize that I hadn't even seen the worst part yet. You have been there throughout every up and down over the last five years. I have never once had to doubt your love for me..." she stops and takes a shaky breath. "When I was drowning and felt like I would never see the surface, you reached in and held my hand until I could find my way back. I will never be able to put into words the joy that you bring to my life, and I can't wait to spend forever with you. I love you, Atticus Michael Reed." Although I try to hold back the tears, a few stray ones fall as Rose finishes her vows.

Once we exchange rings, the officiant clears his throat. "Atticus and Rose, it is my privilege to announce you as husband and wife. You may kiss the bride."

Finally, the moment I have been waiting for since those doors first opened. I slide one arm around her waist, and the other rest on the back of her neck as I lean down and press my lips to hers. Her arms go around my neck and suddenly it's like we are the only two people in the world.

When I reluctantly pull away, the officiant announces, "Ladies and gentlemen, it is my pleasure to introduce to you for the first time, Mr. and Mrs. Reed!"

I steal a quick kiss before I grin down at her. Hand in hand, we walk down the aisle and begin our new adventure as husband and wife.

Acknowledgments

First and foremost, I want to thank my husband, who without a doubt has the patience of a saint. He has always supported me through my crazy ideas and didn't bat an eye when I said I was going to publish a book. He listened to me complain about the plot holes and when I got stuck. Mainly, he never once said I couldn't do it. I'd also like to thank my family for also giving me all the love and support to chase my dreams.

To my friends, Devan, Megan, Melissa, and Kaylee, who endured those awful first drafts and my many edits, y'all are the real MVPs. I'm sure you were relieved when Evan quit blowing up your emails every single night. You never once complained about reading, nor about my constant talk about the book. You're my own little hype team.

Special shout out to Kaylee Beeman with Beauty Bee Branding LLC for always knocking it out of the park on my design requests. This cover was everything I could want and more.

My amazing alpha and beta readers who helped me work through some issues before it went off to publishing. I am so, so thankful for all of you, and I one hundred percent couldn't have done this without any of you.

Made in the USA
Middletown, DE
06 July 2023